Spitting the pips out

Gillian Allnutt

Sheba Feminist Publishers

Spitting the Pips Out first published in Great Britain
in July 1981 by Sheba Feminist Publishers,
488 Kingsland Road, London E8.

ISBN 0 907179 06 1
Typeset in Century 11/12 by Julia at Range Left
Photosetters, 01-251 3959
Printed and bound by A. Wheaton & Co. Ltd., Exeter
Cover Design by An Dekker

For my sisters Jane and Elizabeth

Among magazines and anthologies in which some of these poems have appeared are:

Bananas
Schreiben
(published in
Bremen, West
Germany)
Spare Rib
Spinster
New Poetry
5 (published
1979 by
Hutchinsons in
association
with the Arts
Council of
Great Britain
and PEN)

though Eve
was gullible
she gave us
one thing
more original
than sin

the apple
with its hard
green skin
cannot
be taken in
without
much chewing
or a song

From the Notebook

In the summer of 1978 I wrote a sequence of five poems. Eve is the speaker and she and Adam are old and near the end of their life on earth.

It is never easy to pin a poem down and often this is a bad thing to do to it. A poem speaks for itself and says whatever anyone (including me) finds in it.

For a long time I did not understand the full implications of these five poems, especially the fourth, the one in which something happens to Eve. She dies or she freaks out or God comes to get her. When I was writing them, I planned to make Adam die in that one. I fought with the poem all the time I was writing it, but it refused to turn out the way I wanted. Eve (or the poem) had a will of her own. A year and a half later, when I had an almost-breakdown, I understood what that fourth poem was about.

I wrote the poems because I had a friend who, that summer, I felt sure would commit suicide. (He did, a year later.) I wanted to say to him 'Keep your feet on the ground.' Like Eve says to Adam, 'Stop worrying about God. We've had a good life on earth. It's OK.'

I wrote them also about a relationship with another man I was living in at the time.

Eve was me. Independent, resilient, a survivor. Now I realise that Adam was not only the two men mentioned, or perhaps any man, but also me. The scared, anxious one, the impossible idealist, the one in need of comforting and protection, the one who wasn't any help at all at the moment of crisis.

I have kept the five Adam and Eve poems together and put them at the beginning. In them I can see a development of thought which has helped me shape the book.

The first poem is a celebration of (hetero)sexuality. The first part of the book is an exploration of that.

In the second poem Eve is content but Adam is anxious to get back to the Garden of Eden. He paints. Much of the second part of the book is about writing, which is *my* way of exploring a dissatisfaction with 'reality' and of trying to recover my 'real' self.

In the third poem Eve recalls the struggle and achievements of their life on earth. She chides Adam because he cannot be pleased with that. The third part of the book is about energy, making and doing things, but the last poem, 'winter among the skips', records a sense of disillusion and leads on into the fourth part of the book.

There is a gap between the fourth and fifth poems. The fifth poem is different in style and I wrote it a couple of months after the others.

The fourth part of the book, I think, fills in that gap. For Eve it is the end of her old life. Her old personality won't serve her any longer. She goes down into the dark. And then she begins to come up again.

In the last poem she has regained the Garden of

Eden, but she is alone and happy to be so. She is whole.

The shape I have given this book is to some extent arbitrary. The poems and stories and bits and pieces do not appear in the order in which I wrote them. In some sense it is true to say that they have all always been there. I could have put them together in a number of different ways.

I do not know what truth is. Perception, experience and memory are all shaped by the imagination, which itself has grown out of these three. But all the pieces in this book are more or less closely linked to what I have lived through.

One of the things I want to do is to make the links between writing and living, between particularly the poems and the experience they have come out of. This is because I want to help demystify writing, to share not only the products but also the process, so as to make it something that other women (people) feel they can do too if they want to.

However, I want too to let every piece in the book – and again particularly the poems – float free.

To let them say whatever they say to anyone who picks them up.

Adam
your sapling tree grew leafy in my hand
put down roots in my dark earth
drank of my rain mouth and
flowering out of me
seeded my red blood
grew me an apple

Already I knew
as we stood there sated and uncertain
trying to hide inside our happy bodies
mouths sticky with sweet apple kisses
the core of God's heart forgotten
at our feet   hard bitten
love bites red as a ring of roses on my breasts –
I knew

A great wind grew in the tree
shaking the golden apples like fists
I felt your ribs break
among my budding fingers
your heart beat like a wounded bird
in my hand as you grappled
with God
            Already
I felt the soft rot of the worm
at my ripening heart. Easy
I watched the wind die
down in the leaves of
the crabapple

There were bits of the core between my teeth
I was ready for the hard earth
ready to bring forth
stones   children
stubborn as dead trees
under a heaving sky.   I was ready
for anything
                    for I had known
your shining skin
the sour sweet taste of your tongue
beneath my own
the leaf lift of your breath
upon my breast   the root
of you earthed in me

• • •

Adam paints
the golden apples of the sun.
It is the god in him
gilds the good green shadows
of my garden.

Rain anoints my heart
and I am rooted among
grasses where the wind
stirs gentle in my hair.
I am happy with an
apronful of apples.

Adam peers
among the soft rain shadows
of my tree.
                    His hands are
taut   wet   winter
bare. The wind has bit
into his heart. He tears
my leaves apart
                              to find
God's golden skin
dissolving and dissolving
in the rain.

• • •

Adam
your round cropped head lies
in the shelter of my arm
a small good world
of stone earth trees
walled against wind

How we have worked our garden
out of the hard rock
and the wind and rain
with thin hands learning
to plant and pluck
thin fruit, learning
to eat

You say you are
a windswept garden
unwalled broken
God roams in you plucking
dead leaves from the tree
sucking at windfalls
blames you for having eaten
of my body bitter sweet
and for the small round bowl of fruit
on our rough table
and for the hardy stock of children
ready capable
and for the dry stone wall
we raised around our plot
to keep the wind out

You say God gets
in among the trees
and strips them
                    Adam
your ribs are rough hewn
sturdy as a thorn
against the wind
and your heart is tough
in its brown skin, worn
unbeaten
            Bury your old head
in my hands these sun warmed
stones that nest
in a sheltered corner
of the garden

• • •

I remember
how your hand slid
under my shoulder
held me
as I laboured
in a pain of birth –
our first hard
headed child –
you held me
to your weathered body
rain and wind and stone.

Adam my sturdy earth
bear with me.

God is alone
in a garden without children.
He walks in a dream.
I hardly remember him
now. The delicate rain
bow fades. I only know
I found a golden apple
at the end of it
and ate.

Remember
how I took you
in my mouth
beloved earth
your stones and grass and trees
and how the wind was in you
and you moved me.

Adam my birth
was difficult.

Forgive me
for the first rough
winter. Remember
how I tumbled
among stones
and how your hands
grew round my
stubborn body
fed me wind
and apples.

Adam hide me in your hand
and feed me.

My familiar earth
grows small
                    ephemeral
A rainbow scalds
my mouth
                    I do not know
this ruthless wind that
tumbles me
                    from your side
Give me your
rough hand
                    as I live –

Adam my small earth
rumbles with love.

• • •

this woman
widowed now and unafraid
walks in a garden
on the other side of rainbows

wind is cradled in the air

she has cut off her shadow like hair
and pares her body down
old green skin coils quietly in her hand

she sits alone
at the honey pot of the sun
tells no-one
eats her fill

old husband body is a tree of shadows
laid along the ground to
dry among apple shells

one

One Friday morning of the third term in kindergarten remained cloistered for ever in Eve's memory. No matter how many times she remembered, it would not be dislodged, would never even fade, nor the feeling that went with it.

Two big girls from the top class were brought into the room and placed before the rows of kindergarten baby faces. The two girls' faces were pale and shut behind the great red lips they had smeared around their own small impertinent mouths. Eve gazed at the two white faces with the grotesque smiling red lips and, even though she froze in fear for them and for herself – for the anger of the nuns made the world run cold, anyone could be killed – still she absorbed that day's lesson, blacker and more fundamental than almost any other day's she could remember. Lipstick was a shame beyond utterance, a deeper scarlet than the most cardinal sin, and the only punishment must be a profound humiliation. The two big girls were made to kneel out the morning in front of the tiny table altar with its statue of the Virgin smiling serenely, their backs exposed to the gaze of the forty baby faces bending over sums and small crayonned pictures and looking up for approval again and again.

poem to not the first man

but old adam stands
thumps one closed fist
into the other palm   stamps
up and down the room

dope   wine   aretha franklin
aid and abet the rubbing up
of passion

eve is accessory to all this

taking her place by the hearth
she hands the joint   holds newsprint
in front of the fire
                    to make it draw
the big bold shadow of adam   up wall
and over them both of them

Her deflowering, of course she remembered that – now – though for several years, whenever the scene entered her mind, she had snapped it shut like a compact.

The word by itself made her curl up, close her petals on the secret vulnerable centre of herself, like a flower closing against the cold inroads of a rainy night.

The lily and the rose.

A lily pad sealed the entrance to her womb. It was thick and green enough for a frog to dance on. A white flower grew in silence from the centre of it on a curled green stem. It opened as she grew until its petals spread wide in a many-layered star within her warm vagina. She walked half sleeping, safely sealed off from the world. No-one could get in and she could not get out.

That was the trouble, she wanted to get out. Rapunzel, she let down her hair attractively, walked out with many young men in her first year at college. Some were nice and talked to her respectfully over dinner in a quiet restaurant: but others were rapacious (she learned the word that year), required a grain of truth in the tales they told their roommates over sherry, were out to get it. There were so many of them, it was all very difficult. One of them said 'I shall have to rape you' as they walked across the grass beside the lecture block. But she was fierce and although it was dark he didn't.

She was too fierce and she stifled. She couldn't see beyond the thick yashmak of her virginity. She couldn't breathe.

She refused them all, she went home for the summer holidays, she went to Italy, she determined to discard it there and she did.

Eve lit a cigarette and propped herself up on one elbow. She had to force herself through this story, even now.

It rained and rained in Bologna that weekend. Three days the clouds were down and when they drove back to Florence afterwards he took the mountain road because on the motorway you had to pay a toll and he was too mean and there was fog on the corkscrew mountainsides and they couldn't see a thing yet he drove very fast and one time so nearly smashed into a blue truck on a corner she never knew how he missed it.

So she would recall it, getting to afterwards first, because before the fog mountain Monday drive had been worse.

Then she would go on to the ancient city, what little she remembered, setting her scene laboriously, racking her brains for more details, more picturesque leaning towers, more craftily covered streets (it must rain often in Bologna), more mosaic pavements – anything to draw out the thread of her story a little more before it reached the breaking point. That part always took her as far as the street door of the pensione where they stayed (quietly).

He insisted on silence, at the most a few terse words. He was tense, foul-tempered, brutally purposeful. He was American, a gynaecologist who told her his stock of amusing stories, on the way to Bologna, about the absurd terrors of women, how they wouldn't be probed, how they got strange objects stuck up inside them. She listened in silence. He had come to Bologna to do an abortion, a favour for the Catholic friend of a friend, it would be a kitchen table affair, she was five months gone and if he made a mistake he'd have to take her to the hospital and he himself would be arrested. He was tense and smoked one expensive American cigarette after the other. He was big, hairy, bearded, strong as a bear. He was called Jason for short. He would deflower her as a favour on the Saturday night. They dumped their bags on the two single beds in the high square room in the pensione. It had a marble floor, small mats that slid about, a huge wardrobe, a tiny cracked basin for washing, a bare bulb for the light. There was a patch of grease on the wallpaper above one of the beds. The shutters were half-closed and the light was dim and green. He left her at once, taking the torn scrap of paper with the abortion address and his bag of tools. She went out into the rain and wandered about and bought a paperback. She needed to read and she needed something English and clean. It was *Emma* by Jane Austen, which meant she'd have to concentrate, she'd hated Jane Austen ever since having to read *Northanger Abbey* five times for an exam, she would need all her mind for that subtle stilted language. She lay down on the grey-green counterpane on one of the two narrow beds, she read three pages and then she counted the cracks in the ceiling. For hours. When he came back he was hot and dirty and he hadn't done it. All the family had been there today, tomorrow only the girl and her brother, whose friend had asked him to do it. It would be difficult. He'd told them to scrub the kitchen table, to scour the enamel bowls, to get rags. He lay down on the other bed, he scratched himself, he smoked. Then he said 'Let's get to bed and get it over with. I've got work to do tomorrow. I'll need all the sleep I can get.' While he was out of the room Eve took off her clothes and lay down in the bed beneath the grey sheet, the grey-green counterpane. She watched him peel off his sweat-stained shirt, unlace the heavy workman's boots he travelled in, kick them off, shake down his jeans, strip off his underpants. She watched him through half-closed eyes. 'Move over' he said, thrusting himself into the narrow bed beside her. He was sticky and hot. He rubbed his body against hers. Eve was cool, dry, she made herself 'thin as a pin' (the old gymnasium phrase coming into her head, one of the others was 'wide as a gate'), she pressed her legs together, his hand prised them apart, she tightened them, he forced them. He rolled on top of her, he forced the breath out of her stomach, she gasped, she got her arms free, she struggled to get him off her. He pushed and pushed, it was dry, he pushed more, he was inside her, half in. She fought, he was a dead weight on her chest, she couldn't breathe, she panicked, she cried out 'Stop stop'. He told her to be quiet, the maid would come or the guests in the room next door. She got out 'I can't breathe', her breath coming in short dry gasps. He pushed on and on, he put his hand over her mouth, she couldn't scream. He got there, took the stifling hand away, subsided on her. She gathered all her strength and pushed him off to one side. 'Ungrateful bitch' he said and went to sleep. The next day he did the abortion. He said the foetus was several inches long. He cut it in four and flushed it down the toilet. The girl was all right but weak. She cried and she thrashed about on the narrow table. They had to put her to sleep to make her be still. He was never going to do that again, too much risk. He forced Eve to do it again that night, he said she would have to get used to it.

Eve lay back in bed. She'd got through it again, she couldn't accept it any more than the last time.

And the rose. A wound. And one of the fiercer flowers. She put out her thorns, she wrote 'I am red and I bite.'

I dreamed that my flute was gone

I lost you
thin unbending self.
My hands loosened
lacking the singular shape
of your life.

I wanted to hear you breathing
somewhere still
but a harsh wind scoured my ears
and my tongue was ill with silence.

I plucked at the knuckled hand
of the one
I knew
had abducted you –
soul I had sounded so well –

but he doubled back
and a look bent with laughter
curled on the place
where he must have worked
silent, intent
to conceal you, face down
in the stifling earth.

Last night I held you in my arms as you slept. The room was quiet and the uncurtained window flung its shadow of light wide across the ceiling. A truck roared along the main road, going somewhere, north I think. I was not going anywhere and I was warm. I watched your sleeping face. It was trustful, not taking shape in the frown that always shields it from the world and people like me. I wondered what you looked like as a child, I tried to see. Your body jumped in sleep as if your dream attacked you. I held you closer.

Once my mother dreamed my father kept a knife under his pillow, drew it out and held it to her throat. When she woke up she dared not snuggle up to him for comfort.

That is how it is, old loved enemy, sleeping safe now. But in this small dark time you are my child. Your cheek lies on my breast and your breath comes little, snuffly. You are an animal curled up close, a dormouse in a teapot. But in the morning you will lumber out of this nest of bedclothes, warm tealeaves, stagger off to make coffee, come back up grumbling, spilling it across the untidy floor. My kiss will be sour in your mouth, your tongue will make harsh words, my ears will be scoured of love listening to you.

You sleep now and I remember how I too dreamed once. We went to a big old ruined house. You took me there. We wandered in the overgrown garden, then we climbed the ivy up the wall of the ruined house, to an upper room. I had brought my flute, I don't know why, but I laid it down there while we explored the other rooms in the house. Then there were lots of people, women I knew. It was a party. They said 'Give us some music. Play your flute for us.' I couldn't remember where I had left it. I looked around for you. You were gone. I knew I would not find my flute again until you came back because you had hidden it. When I woke up I knew it was my self you had hidden in that dark room at the top of the ruined house. I kept my dream to myself.

You say I have secrets, your ears grow wider wanting them. You are ugly like a gnome then, hunched as you strain for my words, bend over them, clutch them to your ribs, hoarding them. They are flowers that wither in your greedy bony hands. You must learn to let them grow. There is a garden where you may not go, but I will bring you the fruits of it.

Your hair is soft as seed grasses, gentles my cheek as I kiss you. Your forehead is smooth and warm like an old worn stone in the sun. Your face is furrowed as a field in winter. You are old, I hold an old man to my warm body.

The night is strangely timeless, it is as if I have always known you, always missed you until one day brought us together in the same place. Why did we meet? I have met you sometimes here in this unmade bed, other times I have slept my nights beside you. Why is it you come and go so unexpectedly, wayward one?

I hold you close now, sheltering your sleep, keeping your frail kisses safe under my tongue, holding the nugget of your heart warm in my hand, shielding your skin from the wind with the cloth of my skin.

Last night the shadow of the window crept across the ceiling with the cold moon. It was waiting for morning.

Words to her Lover

I shall keep this bit for God, she said,
tucking it away.

It could be a flower
or a star, a wooden spoon, rice
paper, the shine of the river
a common or garden stone –

You cannot see inside a stone, she said.

It could be a moth
or a stamp with an African bird on it
a word I have forgotten
or a thin cloth folded like a handkerchief
a leaf just looking
or the trick of an eyelid dreaming
a drop of cream, an apple
and a book on a rainy day
a wooden doll with one leg broken since my birthday
or a thread in the eye of a needle.

Desist, she said,
mocking his open fist.

I have given you my bones to keep.
I will sleep like the earth in you.
I've given you my eyes, though they are stones,
my apple heart with its green sleeves.
I'll sing you a song like a river flowing,
give you the sea that grieves in me
like broken things forgotten.
I would stir the earth for you
like a great wind blowing.

But I am going where the moon goes now
when she has finished sewing up the sky
and sits and eats stars
on the other side.

Give me the wooden spoon
so I can eat my curds and whey, she said,
tucking in.

Notebook

Scheherezade told so many stories to save her life.
And the Sultan sat fingering the knife, its glitter
subdued during the moon's uncertain hours,
listening, always thinking he'd find the secret
without having to cut off the beautiful head with
its haunting eyes, so deep . . .

she wiped them
(that were her hands)
on her apron
and said no

flowers falter at that
wet spot where
hands keep wiping
the husband out
of her eyes

no is her mouth
like a bowl licked
clean of a young girl
dipping her finger in grass

the sweet toothed
husband likes angelica
crystallised roses
sugar bright violets
on glass eyed cakes

his hands are
like claw hammers
pulling at fingers
and say not no

he is cutting
bright flowers out
of the apron nailed
to (with wet hands)
the back of the door

Eve was on the stage under a strong yellow light. The lights had been left on in the whole school hall and she could see the rows of parents as she looked up out of the play, forgetting. She saw her mother's bright eyed, anxious face smiling encouragement and mouthing words. She heard another voice singing with her the faltering lullaby she had got halfway through when she stopped. She started singing again, for she was Mary and the baby Jesus was the doll from the wendy house in the classroom that she only got to play in on Friday afternoons and Mother Mary had said to be careful because the head was loose and might come off. She clutched it tight in its white swaddling clothes and sat stiff in the long blue robe to the end of the song.

• • •

She brought out a finger from under the bedclothes. It was covered in warm brown blood. She wiped it on a red square of the tartan blanket that covered her. Her finger was sticky when it touched her thumb.

Her mother had told her what to expect, had had a little talk with her, because a printed letter from the headmistress of the new secondary school had requested that she prepare her daughter. 'We do not want any silliness among our girls.' They sat at the diningroom table one evening in the summer holidays and her mother hesitated on the other side of the vase of roses that dropped their petals on the scratched brown table top. Eve discovered a pin in one of the grooves of the table and tried very hard to get it out. Then she used it to scratch a little heap of fluff and crumbs out of the groove. What she learned was that the world was a man's world, that it was deep bitterness to be a woman.

in my blue room

I wake
with a mouthful of the sky
the blue ache of the infinite
in my bones

I am alone
with the window
and my share
of an awkward
horizon jacked up
on blocks of stone
city sticking
its shards up
into the long suffering blue

and I am in love with you
whom I shut out
of my three white walls
and one blue

I am spare
in soul, shriven
of your tongue
here in this sort of
a cell, the stripped
mood of the nun
upon me, suffering
my one blue wall
in silence

and you
with your shards
of love
cut short

Eve lay in bed feeling the pain roam in her abdomen. She was on her back giving it free play. She couldn't pin it down, locate it in belly, groin or back. It was everywhere, it was taking over. She couldn't get up. Slowly she revolved the lower half of her body, round and round, making love to the pain, trying to appease it. She circled always in a clockwise direction, the other way was jerky, forced, requiring concentration. Why? Was it because she was right-handed or because she lived in the northern hemisphere? Idle thoughts formed an interlude between one round and the next. It came again, a sharp thrust, and she turned on her side, curling up around it, protecting it. She laid the hot water bottle against her stomach, but it was cold and only drew the meagre warmth out of her body. She wriggled her toes, twisted her body, fighting shy, trying to evade it. She writhed, groaned a little, thought of the words 'writhe', 'groan'. Let the pain come out of her mouth, let her cry out. Let her unclench her fists, let it go, escape like a puff of smoke. It relented a moment and she thought how melodramatic it was to moan, or perhaps merely un-British. She flattened her upper lip against her teeth.

october 6th 1980

leafwild the wind
tonight   the rain
the road I am

blown down
to tell you or
you or anyone

hands bewildered
apples   one red
one green

my out of breath
heart a rosehip
holding on tight

this morning
my niece was born
leaf bright

but my redhaired
sister was almost
blown down

The pain returned with a vengeance and she tightened her body all over, making it into a fierce little ball, trying to squeeze the pain out, since it had again forced an entry. Sometimes she poisoned it with an aspirin, but this seemed like cheating, taking unfair advantage. She would only do it when the pain had nearly overcome her, forcing her head down between her knees or revolving her whole stomach so mercilessly around itself that all she wanted to do was throw up her guts and be done. Then she would swallow the acid white pills and await victory, laughing inside, thinking 'Soon you'll be defeated'.

But the grey Puritan martyr, the thin spare saint would speak to her quietly. Almost certainly this saint was a man, and no sensual Sebastian, bleeding luxuriously from every arrowhead, but a sackcloth and ashes saint, a fisherman with no catch, a bread and water vision of John Wesley, prompted to utterance by a cold tap on the shoulder from St Paul, the woman despiser. 'Suffering is good for the soul. Women must expiate the apple.'

Boys will be Boys

Little boy in the garden
why do you never cry?

The sun is always up in the sky.

Suddenly she was cold with child
round and white like the moon.
What do you mean
you didn't know her?
Why did you pretend?
Suddenly she was at an end.

Perhaps at nineteen
you could be forgiven
that quick denial of pain.
At thirty-one

(twelve years of
scuffing your fears
under a stone)

who will forgive you
for playing with pain
like a mud pie
carelessly

for manipulating the moon
and her wet light?

Will you for one moment
forget the delight
of turning away
to another sort of play
merrily?

Little boy in the sun
what is that shadow under the tree?

It is the shadow of a man.

Eve picked out the shape of a womb in the cracks on the ceiling. She added the vagina and a hand inserting a cap the right way up.

They were kind, those volunteer ladies at the clinic, but sensible. They did not believe in nonsense. They always called her 'Mrs' to save themselves, or maybe to save their husbands. Women knew more than they ever let on, at least that generation did. Younger women spoke out boldly now, making demands, refusing discretion. Eve did too, but selectively. At the clinic she was demure and obedient, lying quietly on the sheet of clean white paper on the flat, plastic covered bed, submitting to the practised hand in its polythene glove feeling about inside her.

'A good fit. You're the right shape for a cap. Very suitable,' they said. But, drawing it out and holding it up to the white striplight, they were disapproving. 'What have you done to it? See how it's out of shape. You're pinching it too hard when you put it in. You must bend it back into shape when it gets like this. If it becomes oval, sperm can swim up round the sides.'

Eve looked abashed and gazed at the long thin cap making abrupt movements in mid air. It dropped to the wastebin along with the polythene glove and Eve lay calm on her back thinking about how, if she made love on top, the cap would shift around inside her.

'All right, you can get dressed now,' said the nurse and washed her hands with medical soap in the little washbasin in the corner. In this place, thought Eve, as she pulled up her trousers, sperm were devils, little black villains that swam too well. A whole army of volunteer ladies in white overalls could never be sure of defeating them. There were always one or two that got away. They looked like tadpoles in all the diagrams, but really they were wickedly small and could not be seen with the naked eye, only with one decently protected by the length of a microscope. The nurse wrote numbers on a chart, size and strength, and prescribed two fat tubes of death white spermkiller. Grimly she wrote and dismissed Eve with a fearsome smile. 'Collect these from the desk downstairs.' Eve went down the cold stone staircase in search of new weapons. Women must fight the good fight.

a woman gets a little bit of wisdom

all day yesterday
I walked about in a coat of many colours dream
blown out of a pipe of clay
by him

but today I wrote
an old blue meanie poem
after two nights sleep in one night
and I didn't show it to him

Notebook

When I first began living with him I wrote every evening in my diary, before he came home. I didn't tell him I had a diary. It looked like an old school exercise book. But all I wrote was 'I love him'. So then I went back to my childhood, when I was just me. I wrote about the games we used to play, Sarah and Matty and me, about our runaway children world, about the apple tree, about school, about getting my first period.

two

Notebook

The first writing I ever did wasn't writing at all. It was playing runaway children, mothers and fathers, orphanages. But it was in the same other world. I got the same feeling of excitement as we set up our house under the apple tree in the back garden or our orphanage in the bedroom on a rainy day in the long summer holidays.

The same feeling. A game playing itself out, hurrying us with it to find out the end. A story unravelling itself like a ball of wool that was there in hiding all the time. A poem appearing like broken pieces of an old bowl and letting me put them together again.

That bright kind strange other world took us in. It was always there. It cured us of our boredom. It showed us the rare and wonderful side of ordinary things. It bore with our explorations. It gave us an oddly beautiful terrain where we made our journeys to the interior.

I still go there from time to time, to take my rest, to find myself. It is a garden that God has left behind.

('Let's play runaway children,' suggested Eve.)

Sarah crouched at the foot of her bed, spoke in a small scared voice.

'Why don't Mummy and Daddy come back for us? Why have they left us here with Aunt Mildred? She is so cruel.'

'Yes, she beat me yesterday when I didn't scrub the kitchen tiles properly. She made me do it again,' wailed Matty. 'Why doesn't Mummy come?'

'Sarah, Matty,' said Eve, the eldest sister, 'you know they aren't coming back. You know they got taken away in the war when the Germans dropped bombs on London and we were evacuated to the country.'

(Sarah looked up, surprised out of the game.

'You never said we got evacuated before,' she said accusingly.

'Well, I didn't think of it. Shut up. Let's go on.')

'What shall we do, Eve?' asked Matty pitifully.

Eve put her chin in her hand. The others waited impatiently.

'I know,' she cried, 'we'll run away!'

'Tonight, before supper? I have to peel the potatoes,' said Sarah.

'No, silly, at midnight, when it's dark. We'll tear up our sheets and tie them to the leg of the bed and climb out of the window and down to the ground.'

'Let's pack our cases,' said Matty. 'I'm taking Millie and Gus.'

'Stupid, we're orphans,' said Eve in exasperation. 'We haven't got dolls, we haven't got anything. We're poor and nobody loves us.'

'O, I forgot,' said Matty, almost in tears.

'I pinched a crust of bread from the bin,' whispered Sarah. 'Aunt went out of the kitchen when I was doing the potatoes. I did it fast. I put it in my pocket. When she came back she slapped me because I got some water on the floor. She said girls must learn quicker than that, I'm silly and slow . . .'

'And I saved a bit of sugar from supper,' said Eve. 'Two lumps. I slipped them into my lap when she was pouring the tea.'

Matty burst into tears.

'I haven't got anything!'

'Never mind, Matty,' said Sarah. 'You're only little.'

'You can share our bread and sugar,' added Eve. 'We'll look after you, we won't let you die.'

'Now we've got to escape,' whispered Sarah. 'I've ripped up my sheet.'

'Come on!'

(They stood in the back garden beneath Eve's bedroom window.)

'Phew!' gasped Eve. 'That was a dangerous climb. I thought the sheet would break.'

'I heard a noise when I was halfway down. It was Aunt Mildred going to the toilet,' boasted Matty.

'Gosh, I hope she won't look into our rooms,' said Sarah. 'Come on! We'd better make our getaway quick. We've got to climb over the wall.'

'The spot where the apple tree is,' whispered Eve, already beginning to run. 'You can put your foot on the knob on the trunk. Matty, I'll give you a leg up.'

They were over the wall.

'We have to make our way to the railway line,' said Eve.

'It's a long walk,' said Sarah. 'Do you think we'll make it by daylight?'

'We have to,' said Eve. 'There's a train at half past five. I know, I hear it every morning, just before Aunt Mildred comes to wake us up.'

'But we haven't got any money,' whispered Matty.

'Matty, you can stop whispering now. We're away from the house. And we don't need money. We'll jump the train. Come on.'

(They walked round and round the worn patch of lawn.)

'I'm tired,' declared Matty, puffing.

'We'll give you a ride,' said Sarah.

Sarah and Eve crossed their arms, gripped each other by the wrists.

'Hop up.'

They started walking again.

'Here's the embankment at last!' gasped Eve. She and Sarah loosened their wrists, let Matty down gently.

'I went to sleep,' said Matty proudly.

(They crouched by the rubbish dump.)

'The train will come any minute,' said Eve. 'It goes slowly, it's a goods train. We must grab hold of an open truck and climb up. We can ride on the top.'

'But Eve, why are we going on a train?' asked Matty.

'We're going to Germany,' said Eve.

'To find Mummy and Daddy,' added Sarah.

'I hear a train,' said Matty excitedly.

'Here it comes!' Eve's heart beat hard in her chest. 'Ready?'

'Now!'

(They scrambled up on the rubbish dump. Their bare legs sank into the brambles. They struggled to the top and perched on the brick wall dividing their garden from the neighbours'.)

'I hurt myself,' cried Matty.

'Never mind. We made it,' said Eve unsympathetically. 'Shut up, Matty, there's lots of fine sand to lie in up here.'

'Let's eat the food,' suggested Sarah.

'Now we're in Germany,' declared Eve.

'There's a big forest,' Sarah pointed. 'No-one will see us in there. Let's jump down.'

'OK.' Eve prodded Matty. 'Come on, it's time to get off.'

(They jumped off the wall, clearing the rubbish dump.)

'Quick! The guard might see us! Run to the trees!' gasped Sarah.

(They ran to the apple tree, crouched beneath it.)

'We've got no time to lose. We must get out of the forest before nightfall or we'll get lost and be wandering here forever till we die,' said Eve. 'Come on.'

They walked and walked.

('Dinner time, girls!' called their mother from the kitchen window. 'Come in and wash your hands now, please.')

'Look!' said Eve quickly. 'There's a cottage in that clearing. Maybe the old woman will give us something to eat.'

(The old woman gave them shepherd's pie and peas, with treacle tart and custard for pudding.)

Eve thanked the old woman.

'You can all stay here as long as you want,' she croaked. 'I'm all alone. I'd like some company.'

'O no, we have to find our mother,' said Eve.

'And Daddy,' piped up Matty.

(But Sarah said,

'Eve, let's stay. It's nice here. And anyway I'm tired of this game. Let's play something else.'

'O you always get sick of things so soon,' said Eve crossly. 'You're just stupid.'

'So are you,' returned Sarah.)

Notebook

Even then it was a question of being orphans. The point was to wriggle out of what we were going to have to be. Twenty years later the point was still to escape. To find ourselves.

The Porch at Home

I have sat here before
on the settling step where the ground rises up
in welcome of dust and grasses.
The tired flowers meet above my head
nodding like uncles discussing a change of
    investment.

I am small as a human being faced with a choice of
    stars,
laying my paper seeds among the weeds beside the
    door.
But still my mother sees that she can set no store by
    me:
I only bring her words.

Holding the skein of wool before her eyes
I hear her click her tongue like needles
at the knots and tangles
I have made of the teasing ticklish thread.
'Keep still now, please, don't wriggle.'
She winds her life about the spindle of her hand
and makes a ball the cat can wink at
and that's all.
But she has bound me like a chair
and I must read aloud
my words that sidle in the sultry air of afternoon.
Their shapes hold shadows she will never see:
like cups of tea and currant buns, they're gone
before the stars appear.

Her soul is contained as the carefully folded hands
of virgin aunts.
Nothing can touch
as, inadvertently, her needle puts the moon's eye
out.
She knits, quite unsuspicious
of my search for the one lost stitch.

My seeds are sixpences the great aunts gave
when stars were only teatrays in the sky.
But I have buried them.
She only sees the heads of queens, beheaded now.
I watch my words not grow here
set in this thrifty earth,
its pores like stones, close-fisted,
stinting light.

The shapes of words are shadows in the moonbright
air
that flee like ghosts from the lair of
the eternal enchanter she called God.
Blind as a clod of earth, unsown,
she sits and closes stitches one by one.

Silent, I shall walk down to the narrow garden gate
knowing I must leave her looking still for Eden
in the pictures of a willow pattern plate.

Notebook

'That's hard,' the women say. They shake their heads over it. Me at the garden gate, saying goodbye. They won't let me leave like that.

My mother and me. What have we denied one another?

These words are hard on me. They won't come out with it. Wooden dolls with their mouths shut tight. Obdurate as a line of therapists. 'Do it yourself. We're not going to tell you. Go home and find out.'

It's no good going home again.

My mother has God, three daughters, a husband, a home and garden, and she knows what is going to happen or not happen next in her life.

I have me and words and a determination not to know about tomorrow.

But where are her poems? Where is she? And where are my children?

'The Porch at Home'. I have tried to square it with her. We have written letters about it. 'I'm glad,' she said, 'I know just what you mean. It is a portrait of my mother. If I could write, I would have put it just like that. Just how I felt. She never understood. Poor Gran, she never did have much imagination.'

And yet my grandmother did so well with her

needle. She could put the whole of the Suffolk countryside onto a tablecloth.

Mothers and daughters. What is the matter with us? How do we miss one another?

'Listen,' I will say to the women – and perhaps they will unbend – 'I had to write that poem. It was a bit of finding out. About what my mother chose to do without. And what I have chosen to do without. Neither of us can bear it. Her imagination is shut up inside her. My children are still shut up inside me. We make one another remember what we have each tried so hard to forget. Why have we had to forget? Since I wrote the poem I have understood how important it is that we do not take out on one another the bitterness of having to do without, to forget; that we both come to know how that forgetting has been forced upon us. Then we can work together so that our daughters and granddaughters may remember everything.'

My wooden doll words have become kind women.

Perhaps, the day after tomorrow, I will go home again.

'When you are born,' said Miss Skinner, 'your soul is like a clean white tablecloth. But when you commit a sin –' Her small eyes looked meaningfully from behind thin glasses with scrolled frames at the class of small girls. 'Eve, what are you doing? Bring that to me.'

Eve had chewed the cushion tip from her hairgrip and had begun bending back one end of the stiff piece of metal. She had to get up from her place halfway down the row and walk to the teacher's desk at the front of the room. She was already afraid, ashamed of being singled out, not daring to think about what was happening.

'Give it to me,' said Miss Skinner in a tight voice, holding out a long white palm.

Eve placed the hairgrip in it.

'I'll teach you not to fidget in my lessons . . . And what have you got in your mouth?' Her eyes narrowed, gleamed. The sharp nose moved pointedly nearer Eve's face.

Eve took out the tiny piece of chewed plastic. It wasn't a sweet.

'Put it in the bin and go back to your seat, you naughty girl. And take a conduct mark.' Miss Skinner, holding back the anger in her bones, opened a drawer, took out the register and made a red mark beside Eve's name, pressing hard.

Eve sat down and folded her hands on top of the desk. Her face burned. She knew she would not feel right again for a long time. However many green stars she gained for good work in the next ten days, she would not be given the 'Merit' badge. She was a clever girl, and too afraid not to be well-behaved, so she often wore the badge pinned to the front of her tunic. It was crest-shaped and purple with 'Merit' printed diagonally across it, in gold between two gold lines. They would say she had let down her house, too, but she hardly cared about that. It was her own pride that was hurt. And she was afraid, too, knowing that the memory of this afternoon's lesson would come back and come back, burning her cheeks a vivid red. The other little girls, still in a state of grace, turned again to face the front, realising the excitement was over, and prepared themselves to hear more about the fate of the soul.

Miss Skinner crossed one spindly leg over the other and her long, tightly pleated grey skirt rearranged itself above her black high-heeled shoes. She folded her hands on top of the register and the knuckles were white. Her cardigan was bright pink and she wore it every day.

'When you commit a sin,' she repeated, putting a meaningful emphasis on the last word, 'your soul is marked.' She paused for effect, then went on, quietly, insinuatingly, her voice entering snake-like into the forty-four young souls that she held in thrall – for ten minutes more until the bell would ring and let them loose upon the wide sinful world. Her words slid in sideways. 'You know what happens if you spill a cup of coffee on a clean white cloth . . .' Her voice rose in triumph. 'The stain is there for ever. However many times you wash the cloth, it won't come out.' Her eyes bored into the forty-four small pale faces fixed on hers. 'And when your soul is stained, God doesn't love you any more. And you will go to Hell when you die and burn for ever.'

The bell rang. They waited until her eyes released them.

'You may stand up now.' They rose together and stood beside their desks. 'Good afternoon, girls.'

'Good afternoon, Miss Skinner,' they chorused

in a single singsong voice.

'Mary, lead out.'

As she waited for the red trolley bus to glide up and take her away from the gates of the convent, Eve puzzled over the tablecloth. She wanted to stop herself from remembering the humiliation of being scolded in front of the whole class. But she was genuinely puzzled, for she had never thought her soul looked like a tablecloth. She knew it was made of the shiny white stuff that was used to stiffen her father's shirt collars, the gleaming strip of plastic that appeared when the collar got old and frayed and needed turning. You could pull it out of the hole in the material and keep it. Eve had one in her treasure box, a flat tin that smelled of tobacco, which she had begged from her father's collection on the garage windowsill. The shiny white stuff could never be stained with coffee – you would simply wipe it clean. It could be put out of shape when the iron was too hot: but that was the worst that could happen to it.

That night Eve got the shiny white strip out of the tobacco tin that lived under her bed. She stole down to the kitchen and quietly reached up for the box of matches on the shelf by the cooker. She lit one and held it to the plastic.

'Eve! What are you doing down here? I sent you to bed hours ago.' It was her mother whose sharp ears had detected the small scratching noise of the match on the side of the box. 'And how many times have I told you not to touch matches? . . . What *are* you doing?' she asked curiously, coming nearer.

'I've hurt my soul,' answered Eve, laying the burnt out match on the kitchen table.

Dear Sarah,

I'm glad you liked the story. It is interesting that you are convinced Miss Skinner's cardigan was black. I know it was a shocking pink. Still, no matter – both are sinful colours. And I suppose she could have got a new one by the time you arrived in Form 1.

It is strange what truth is when you are writing. I used two or three separate incidents from convent days in that story, yet it seemed to me as I was writing it that everything really happened like that. The story took over from my memory. It has an emotional truth rather than a factual one. Someone had hurt me very much, so that I hardly knew what to do with myself. I went to my room and the story came to me and after it was down on the paper I felt much better. But still I do not fully understand its meaning.

Do you think there is anything in it for anyone else? Do you think people will dismiss it with 'What a strange little girl, what an odd story'? If only I could feel that my experiences and what I make of them in writing are worth sharing. If only I knew that other people would identify with my heroine, find some part of themselves in her, see themselves or someone they know more clearly because of her – then I would be sure that what I am doing is not sheer egoism.

Write soon and do not stop painting. After all perhaps the others do not matter very much. It is just important that we should understand ourselves.

Lots of love
Eve

Eve had got rid of God.

But God crept back into her bones, digging His thin dry fingers between her shoulder blades.

It was the fault of Dostoevsky, mainly, who chased God all through the hundreds of pages of his novels, but allowed so much sceptical soul-searching, so much barbarous sin on the way that she felt, maybe the getting back to God made for quite a colourful life after all. It put some light and shadow into the world.

And then it was Gide, too, who wrote with so much clarity and sympathy about Dostoevsky and was looking generously for God in his own books too. He told her to read the Bible as a set of metaphors.

Before that they'd all said it was a story.

Great Uncle Joshua had given her a book on her seventh birthday. It was called 'In the Steps of Jesus'. She never read it but it was a hardback with a dustcover with a photograph of Jerusalem on the front. It carried authority and had pride of place in her childhood bookcase. She had always thought of Jesus as a real man walking and getting his feet dirty. What else was Mary Magdalene's beautiful hair for?

Later she found she couldn't swallow the story.

But now, disguised as a metaphor, God came back,

tricking her, saying *I am the Word*. Words were her undoing. He knew that. He made the Evangelist write the first chapter of John to puzzle her all her life long. He beckoned to her across deserts of blank white paper, laying His trail of temptations. *God* He said and *soul spirit immanence devil tree garden serpent apple*. Wouldn't you like to understand by eating these words and loving them? They are keys to the beautiful secret garden. I have buried them deep beneath the stone of your heart.

And He had. The more she wrote poems, the more she found these holy words slipping in, unobtrusive, usually in the middle of a sentence, almost always in the lower case (even *god*).

The room was cool and had a green carpet. There were big old glass-fronted cupboards along one wall where the few surgical instruments he needed were kept. Reference books full of the new-fangled drugs they kept producing these days were stacked on a small table near the desk.

A girl walked in hesitantly and sat down opposite him.

'And what can I do for you?' The benign surgery voice was calm.

'The muscles in my stomach ache and ache,' explained Eve.

'Oh?' said the old doctor in his slow monotone. His way was kindliness even though there were now so many patients on his books there was hardly even time to be efficient. Probably there was very little wrong with this young girl, but he would listen with half an ear. He laid down his pen on the big leather-topped desk, folded his hands and looked at her in attentive concern.

He was tired. Women came to him every day with their small worries. They were healthy normal women with husbands and children, nothing else in the world to keep them awake at night, and yet they came. He would never understand. His own wife had died a year after the birth of their still born son. He was a doctor and he did not know why she had died.

'Perhaps,' he suggested gently, 'you have been lifting something heavy? Have you moved any furniture lately? A wardrobe or a table?'

'No,' replied Eve.

'Could it be your periods?' he asked. 'Do they

come regularly? Do they cause you much pain? I can give you something for that.'

Eve was doubtful.

'It aches all the time,' she said.

'Are you happy?'

Eve did not understand this question and said nothing.

'I can prescribe some tablets to help you sleep.' He picked up his pen, unscrewed the top with its dull steel shine, pulled the prescription pad towards him, prepared to make his usual small inscrutable lines and dots on the form. He glanced at the medical card in front of him: she was older than she looked, this young girl, still very pretty, not yet married. Perhaps that was it.

'I laugh all night in my dreams,' she was saying.

'Good, good, no nightmares, eh?' He looked up, smiled at her in his fatherly way.

'And all day long I am laughing inside,' she insisted.

He inscribed her name on top of the form, crossed out 'Mrs.', leaving the 'Miss' exposed.

'Got a boyfriend?' he inquired without raising his eyes from the medical card.

Eve was bewildered for a moment.

'I can't stop laughing because the world is absurd. No-one will take me seriously when I point this out to them. No-one listens when I try to explain: they just repeat the story my mother told me at bedtime from the time before I was too young to understand. I still don't understand this story, it doesn't make sense. I have no place in it. They show me my place again and again, but I can't step into it. And then they say I am stubborn and they go off and do something else. But I know that their story is wrong, untrue. They are deluded, they are foolish and I have to laugh at them.

'Now I have studied their story, studied it long

and hard. I have seen what I have to do to fit into the action, to make their plot come out right – and I do it. But I cannot forget that I am acting a part in their tale and I laugh at myself for doing it well – I am not untalented – and I laugh at them for believing me. And so there is no end to this terrible laughter and I . . .'

The doctor stopped writing, laid down his pen, tore the top sheet off the prescription pad, folded it and handed it to her across the big desk. Eve stretched out, took it and put it away in her handbag.

'Take one at night just before you go to bed. Drink some hot milk if you like, to wash it down. I have given you enough for two weeks. If things have not got better by then – if your muscles still ache' – he half smiled – 'then come back for some more. But I'm sure these will do the trick.'

'Thank you,' said Eve meekly and got up and went.

The doctor stared at the door as it closed quietly behind her. And then what she had said – what he had half overheard as he wrote out the formula he wrote for so many anxious women these days – began to come back to him. But he shook his head as he got up to wash his hands in the large old-fashioned basin in the corner.

'Laughter,' he said to himself. 'That's a new one. Usually they tell me they can't stop crying!'

You Reading My Death Poem At Breakfast

Not my cup of tea, you said,
seeing a shadow under the saucer
shovelling death with a spoon.
Pass me the butter.

You are brown as an egg
unspeculating, spreading
butter like sun.

Why are you creeping under a stone, you said.
It is too soon, too soon
in the day for that.
Life is too short.

The sun is a simpleton.
I have swallowed a cup of hard stars,
gallstones.

But butter would melt in your mouth, you said,
patting my head, smashing the top off
my speckled egg with
a brash spoon.

Notebook

All my old diaries are there – blue notebooks, orange, hardback brown, loose pieces of file paper, all bundled together and stored in plastic garden refuse bags under the table in my old bedroom at home. My mother dusts them now and again. I doubt whether she ever looks inside. Being a woman, she understands the need for secrecy. Everything that fails in 'femininity' lives in a box or a tattered notebook, at first under the bed and later . . . For twenty years she had no time for secrets of her own, because of the washing mainly, also because of the three daughters who from time to time were unhappy at school and the husband who closed up like a stone. But one year she quietly went back to her notebook.

Kitchen Table Woman

It says on the ordinary stone
that she was dearly loved.
Of course she was
                    the soft wet
flesh giving way in his hands
and her hands kneading and mending
for him and several little ones.

But what are these bones
that kept so quiet
beneath the many coloured blouse
and skirt, the pretty petticoat,
the pink white skin?
What is this sardonic skull
that watched beneath her careful
cap and curls and never let
the pretend world in?

Here in her silent room
of unfinished wood
                    she has suffered
the patient unpicking of cloth and skin –
those sweet nothings they buried her in –
and now for the first time notices
her funny indifferent bones.
She scratches her knobbly skull
and knows there is no need to smile
at herself.
          Alone she is able
to let the earth come in and
rain and the little scrabbling life
of the dark.

Out of the interstices of
her bones the rough roots come,
their green shoots hidden, prepared
for the hard stride up to the sky.
The round bowl of her skull
already holds a bulb, unfolds
the tall bold colours of a flower.

Digging In

My house is a wooden ark.
I have tied it with a rope
to the old great oak that has sheltered many
winters,
gathering wind, shadows, slips of the cold sky
in its strong comfortable arms. Earth is warm in
there.
It is wriggling. Later it will come to leaf.

This is my table, old round stump
hefted and heaved
in over the ridged step.
Here I shall set my cup and plate –
leaving my small stains, coffee rings
on the great rings of its many skins –
and the salt pot at the heart of it.

All day I sit licking my animal fingers
watching for sun. It comes
to taste the earth, to know what is there in winter.
Lowering a beam, it finds out dust
discovers the air's visibility
its hopeful imperfections.

It has all been there in hiding
like poems pressed between pages of books
compacted to paper.
There is an oak in a thin paper book
that remembers the wind
the great swell of rain
the weight of snow that made it sleep
and wake wrapped in a new skin.

Through the long night spirits creak
packed hard into the joists.
The wind has woken them.
Their voices crack with cold,
fragmented. There are awkward
shadows cut out by the candle.
They have not had their fill of light.
Embittered, thin, they batten on
the small knot of my winter heart
until my store of light and fat is nearly gone.
They are paper knives, the sawn off edges of the soul,
incurable –
Or, if I trim the wick
and let the candle cradle all the air,
will they still leap to sharp conclusions,
still cut the light with their quick hurts?
Perhaps they'll file back quietly to the dark recesses
settle there and smile
among the accommodating arms of the kind roof tree.

What must I take unto myself
through the long hard flood of winter
to share with me my small hearth
melting a great weight of snow for water?

This is my hard chair
and this the great block of wood I whittle at
shaving the many skins from my obstinate soul
with its hidden knots, its splinters
the raw hopeful look of it, rough cut, flawed –
I run my thumb along the newly whetted knife edge,
cut into the grain of wriggling life
and shape a tree.

three

I wanted somewhere to keep my favourite books. I had a perfectly good bookcase, a birthday present, smooth polished oak, a moveable shelf, sliding glass doors. It wasn't quite what I would have chosen. I didn't like the glass doors, but my father said they would stop the books getting dusty. I would have preferred rough planks with bricks in between.

Occasionally the greengrocer would give you a tomato box if you asked. One day I went shopping for my mother and bought many things and had no bag with me. The man fetched a box from the back of the shop. I had accomplished the first part of my secret plan. I went to Woolworths and bought a tin of dark brown furniture paint. And a brush. I crept into the garage while my mother was sleeping after lunch. I wrestled with the metal handle on the box, twisting and cursing and scraping my knuckles. I finally got it off, even the tacky bits that swivelled round and round the nails attaching the handle to the wood. I stole a screwdriver, guiltily, knowing I would be bound to spoil it. Then I broke the two pieces of wood making one side of the box, smashing them in the middle with my heel. I carefully extracted the splintered ends. I levered open the paint tin (also with the screwdriver) and began to cover the box with big luscious swipes of chocolate brown paint. The smell stung my nostrils, the brush stained my fingers. Carefully I upended my box, painted the bottom. It was done. I opened several of the old tobacco tins on the garage windowsill before I found one containing nails of the right size. I extracted four. I put the tins back in the order I had found them.

Impatiently I did something else. I could not settle all the time the box was drying. At last it was just not sticky. I carried it through the house and up to my bedroom, held it to the wall above my bed and hammered in the four nails. When I took my supporting hand away, the box slipped forward, the nails were rather loose, the wall felt crumbly. But I pushed the box back, I didn't want to see the enormous holes I must have made in the not very old wallpaper. I put some books on my shelf. It stayed up. I was so pleased. I crept back to the garage and replaced the hammer.

When my father came to kiss me goodnight and saw what I had done, I could tell he wasn't pleased. But he could tell that this wasn't a thing to be angry about. So he sent me to fetch the hammer and more nails. When I returned he had taken my box off the wall and was fingering the torn paper round the nail holes. He taught me how to bang along the wall and listen for a solid sound. My knocks were hollow – then came a doubtful one. I looked at him, he nodded, I knocked again. It was a dense matt sound. He said there was a joist there and I could hammer in the box. We put two nails in, one up top and the other at the bottom. It was firm on the wall. But it wasn't right above my bed any more. I was allowed to move the bed.

East Anglian Progenitor

My great grandmother
lost the spouse who had walked by her side
coming back from the malthouse
                                        which was hot
over the wide fields of snow
one night he took pneumonia
and died.

She beat ten children into adulthood.

With a silver crested stick
she tapped her temper to the sticking point
prodded the clods of broad brown fields
to make them productive
wielded the farm on the end of a doughty rod
never took sick but sat up at night
by her furrows of figures
ploughed profit back into the land
made good.

She held each daughter at a needle's end
until she pricked her fingers to the bone
and learned to use a thimble.
And the sons, her favourite ones
                                        when ripe
were put out to apprenticeship.

She discouraged the doubtful bombardier
who courted the eldest daughter
with a rustle of bombasine
and a stick of a smile
                                        a spoke
in the broad blue wheeling sky
of his world.

                    'Toy soldiers' she muttered
churning the milk of motherly love into butter
beating the thousand petticoats to a bloodless
    white
kneading the bread.

East Anglican, great crested glebe
she drove her brood along the straight road
to the Church doors, stiff with Sunday.
Divers sinful country birds fell quiet.
                                                            They heard
her stubborn body snap and click over the frozen
    ruts
and the stick rapped
                                    to the hard earned glory of God.

Eve had a sudden idea on the way back from the shops and the feeling of boredom went away.

'Let's play orphanages,' she said to Sarah.

'All right,' answered Sarah rather dubiously. She always got the broken shoe-boxes for *her* dolls' beds and the smallest hankies for sheets.

'Shall we let Matty play too?'

'We'd better, or Mummy will get cross.'

So they set up rows of small beds along two walls of the room that Eve and Matty shared.

'Why can't we have the dormitory in *my* bedroom?' asked Sarah.

'We can't. You know it's not big enough. We'll have the doctor's room in there.'

'What can *I* do?' demanded Matty, watching her elder sisters busily making up beds.

'Go and find all the dolls' clothes you can from the toy cupboard,' ordered Eve. And Matty trotted off downstairs.

They gathered all the dolls together: Daisy, the baby doll with one finger missing; Elinor, the 'real' baby doll who could be fed water and made to cry tears and wet her nappies if her tummy was pressed in; Bertha and Molly, the tall stiff walkie-talkies whose hair could be plaited and replaited; Annette and Annabelle, the diminutive blonde twins with identical sets of home-made clothes; Freda, the soft rubbery one with bright blue eyes; Singing Bear who gave a rendering of 'Rock a bye Baby' if you pressed his tummy; and Pink Jenkins, so named because very early on his ear had fallen off and this had reminded their father of the War of Jenkin's Ear; Betty and Lucy, the fair and dark rag dolls; Millie and Gus and lots of others who were less favoured, less often washed and combed and kissed.

They took off all the dolls' clothes and stood them on the landing outside the bedroom door.

'Sarah, give them tears now. Get some water from the bathroom. Quick!' commanded Eve. So Sarah put drops of water on the rows of round plastic cheeks.

Then they all went into the bedroom and shut the door and Matty said,

'I can hear crying.'

'No, not yet, Matty, we're not ready yet. Here, get me some books from under your bed to make a table.'

Matty sulked but fetched three big annuals and took them to Eve. Eve stood up, stood still, said,

'What's that sound at the door?'

They went and opened the door and uttered exclamations of surprise and pity and gathered up the dolls and took them in. They were busy for the next two hours, washing, dressing, comforting, putting the dolls to bed.

'Ssh,' whispered Eve and tiptoed out. The others followed.

They got paints and paper and sat at the dining room table and made quantities of food: bacon and fried eggs, slices of meat, round brown potatoes, splotches of greens, currant buns, banana jelly, patches of custard. They waited for them to dry and laboriously cut them out. Sarah's tongue hung out of her mouth in concentration.

Then they gave the orphans a nourishing meal, sitting them up at tables but still in their nighties, as it was the first night.

In the night one orphan got sick and died. Next morning Eve put little blobs of white paste in the rosebud mouths of the dolls and they all had diphtheria and then had injections and began to recover. More nourishing paint and paper dishes were prepared: pools of beef broth, big speckly eggs, pieces of junket with pencil dot nutmeg.

The orphanage sustained a solid and sober existence for the next two days, the matron and staff working their fingers to the bone for the benefit of the fifteen or twenty bedraggled orphans. There was school in the mornings and a sleep after lunch; mass visits to the doctor for polio injections done with a darning needle; expeditions to the garden to play in the sun on the swing. Orphans were naughty and had to be punished or they were inconsolable, wanting their long lost parents and in need of special attention. There was a long and involved bedtime story.

But on the following morning when the orphans were lined up at the hairdressers', Eve cut too much blonde hair off Sarah's favourite doll. A quarrel broke out, they scratched one another and pulled each other's hair.

So the orphanage had to close down.

I first came to the room when it was dark. I brought a bicycle lamp with me. One of them came down the uneven stairs after me. I shone the lamp in front of his feet. Then I shone it in mid air in front of us. He showed me the corner where they'd taken away the old wood panelling. 'It was full of dry rot' he said. Now there were bricks, a raw dull red and patched with damp. He dragged an unwieldy length of hardboard from the French windows. I saw they wouldn't shut together because they were swollen with rain. Six squares of glass were gone. There was a hole in the ceiling, black, ragged round the edges with broken off laths and bits of crumbling plaster waiting to drop down. There was an old gas fire with one and a half of those asbestos pipes that channel the flames up, left. 'But the gas works' he said hopefully. The room smelt rotten. There was a large patch of something unidentifiable and sticky in the middle of the floor. 'But the floorboards are whole.' I said it was a good thing it was so dark and the bicycle lamp batteries were running low.

The next time I came it was a Sunday afternoon, about four o'clock. It was January, so it was already quite dark. He came down the dim staircase. Inside the room I shone the lamp for him. He took out a mains tester and put it to the inside of the light switch. It lit up. He screwed on the round white cover and ran upstairs for a bulb. When he put it in, the light worked. I felt helpless. Later I discovered that every time I touched the light bulb and made it swing (it hung rather low from the low ceiling on a long frayed wire) the light went out at the extremities of the pendulum. I was pleased, I thought I would try to fix it. (I did, three months later.) But I rather liked the cantankerous old wire, I had to treat it with tact, walking carefully past it, back and forth, holding my breath. He wouldn't have understood that.

The next time I came was on a sunny Thursday morning. I had borrowed a plane from a sculptor. It was a beautiful tool, very old, the handle was warm in my palm. The sculptor had assured me it was just the job. But I was afraid they would laugh. 'Fancy thinking she could plane a door with that little thing.' The angle of the blade could be adjusted. I had to guess. I set to work at half past nine. I opened the French windows to the fresh cold air and squatted on the flagstones in the area. I had to clear a space in the thick bed of last autumn's leaves that had drifted down there to die. I looked up at the sky through the black bare branches of the plane trees in the street above me. Then I scraped at the bottom of the doors to shorten them so that they would fit over the sill. It wasn't easy. First I scraped at one door, then at the other, then I went back to the first. My wrist ached with cold and the awkward angle I worked at. A thin line of tiny splinters and shavings appeared on the ground. At half past ten I knew I was getting nowhere. No-one was in the house. I fetched a dirty chair from the kitchen and stood on it to reach the top of the doors. That was better. Bigger slices of wood curled up from under the plane. After a while I tried closing the doors. I could see that now they would slide in easily at the top. But it was a quarter to twelve. In exasperation I attacked the bottoms of the doors again, cut my finger, jammed the plane in a splintery knot. He walked into the room, fresh with the bright morning. 'Why don't you plane the door frame instead of the doors?' He took the plane in his strong square hand, drew it hard along the sill. A thick slice of clean white wood curved up easily. He applied the tool again and again in the same way. In another ten minutes the doors swung to easily and I fastened them with the rusty old bolt.

The next time I came to mend the windows. I had put in panes of glass before, I felt better about this bit, but soon I discovered I had forgotten how to do it, it was seven years ago. He lent me a glazing tool to get out the splintery bits of glass stuck in the hard dry putty in the groove of the frame. The tool was a sharp, delicate triangle of metal specially designed to get in the corners. I also had a kitchen knife with me, I felt more at home with that. I measured up for the new panes with a tape measure from my sewing box. I was impatient. I measured up and then I scraped a bit more putty out. I got the six new panes cut in the shop and carefully carried them home and they were half a centimetre too wide. I went away for three days and then I had to come and get those panes and take them back to the shop. The man was unusually nice and hand-cut away the unwanted half centimetre and I did not have to flutter my eyelashes, only thank him and he didn't charge me for this delicate piece of work which took him all of twenty minutes to carry out, breathing hard in the workshop at the back. After that the windows went in all right. They are still there, though it took six months for the putty to harden in that damp place.

He mended the hole in the ceiling. I held the tape and handed it to him. Then I put my foot on one end of a length of hardboard while he sawed it through the middle. I gave him the hammer and he knocked in three nails. I tried to knock in the other six nails and discovered that when mine went in, his came out. I got him to have a look and he did the rest of the hammering. After he had done the job we agreed that I should have done much more of the work than I actually did. He said he hadn't really known what to do, he was just guessing. I thought the hardboard looked a mess, I would have done it differently, but I didn't know how, and at least the old plaster wasn't falling down any more.

Again I came and covered the bare brickwork with cement. He lent me an oblong flat metal tool with a handle set square to the metal plate. It was the tool meant for the job. I got on well. By chance I mixed the cement to just the right consistency. I seemed to know how to spread it on the wall without seeing it drop straight off again. It was lovely and smooth, though I had to score it so that the next layer of pink plaster would stick to it. Now my cement is cracking and coming away from the walls in thick crumbling lumps, but that is only because the room has dried out so much.

After that, whenever I came, I knew what I was doing. I had scraped, plastered, sanded, painted, scrubbed many times before. I ended up with a bare damp yellow walled basement room and I was still looking for a carpet four months later. It was a room of my own. My mother was upset and said 'Darling, why must you live in these dreadful places?'

Dear Aunty Mildred,

Thank you very much for the bath cubes. (The ones you sent me last year are still in the bathroom cupboard.) I love lily-of-the-valley. It makes me feel so pretty to smell like a flower. (Actually I don't bath very often. There isn't time now I've started the bricklaying course. Also there's no point, I only get dirty again straight away.) And thank you for the soap. I am saving it for special occasions when I want to feel confident and look my best. (I said Sarah or Matty could have it. I didn't even try to swop it, I wanted to *give* it to them and they wouldn't take it.) And thank you for the tights. That dark shade of brown really does something for my legs. (I suppose I *could* wear them up under my overalls on site. It gets really cold in the winter.)

We had a lovely Christmas. I went home this year and Matty was there too – quite a family gathering. It was only a pity Sarah had to spend this Christmas with the in-laws. (It was all right until after lunch on Christmas Day. Then that old feeling of fifty-two Sundays rolled into one hit me. I watched them slumped in the armchairs sleeping off their Christmas pudding. I argued with Matty – well, she *was* darning her boyfriend's socks. She cried, I felt bad about that. And then they switched the television on . . .)

I hope you had a good Christmas too. It was a pity you couldn't come over on Boxing Day after all. Why does the car always have to break down at the most inconvenient times? (If you had come, I couldn't have worn my overalls all day and fixed the radiator in my van. I would have had to hear about the relatives, all your other nieces and their babies, I would have had to wear a dress, maybe even the tights you gave me.)

I do hope you will have a pleasant year. Have you made any marmalade yet? I'm afraid I lost the recipe you sent me last year. (I *think* I used it to start the fire, but maybe someone lined the bin with it. I don't know – I didn't even realise it was gone until my mother wrote asking for it.) Very careless of me. I have made a New Year's Resolution to stop losing everything. Granny always used to say little girls should be tidy and remember to say please. (I do wish you could see my room. Getting to work by eight o'clock every morning leaves me no time to clear up. I need a wife just like you, dear aunt.)

I must stop and wash my hair (change the washer on the tap in the bathroom). Thank you once again for your thoughtful present. (It could raise my chances in the marriage stakes. Isn't that it, aunt?)

With much love (and a spanner in the works to you),

Eve

the benign lady goes berserk one afternoon

mild
as tea with more than a dash of milk
the lady from the Guild

her gentle afternoons
embroider hassocks. thus she avoids
the inconvenience of going out in the rain

flowers neat as a perm edge the cameo horizon
waves lap correctly at an ark
tidy as a powder compact

exactly so and no mistake
the roses at the vicarage
are more tea golden and Dorothy Perkins
than ever before my dear
it must be the rain

suddenly one rolled gold curl
tumbles with the impermanence
of a wave

the ark hits ararat
like a dropped compact

shards of her neat reflection everywhere
on the vicar's parlour floor.

stumble out of the frenzied needle's eye
these fresh unmended animals
fantastical four legged
four threads thick inventions
of the child God

they gobble the vicar's trellised horizons

Garret

At the literary party
I all of a sudden want to go home
to my garret.

'O, a figment of the romantic imagination'
I laugh, but
it isn't that.

It was badly plastered
when I came to it
and drank five litres
of cheap white paint
and refused to give up
the ghosts of its old stains.
It had always liked
to let the rain
that wanted a place to dry in
come in.

The window was prepared
to share the sky
with nextdoor's tumbledown
chimney pot and the odd
bird that sat on it
lost in a smart city.
To the bird it said 'Sing'
and to the reluctant sun
it said 'Come in.
I will give you a shadow or two
though there is little
enough to let slip
between the bare walls
and the low ceiling
of my imagination.'
It let dust come to rest
on the narrow outside ledge.

And it let me come in
with my ordinary tools
hammer and nails and
bucket and cloth cut
from an old pretty skirt
and brushes one fat one thin
and blue and white
pots of paint.

To me it said
'When you are done with
your handyman housewife bit
sit down and write.
I will give you little
but silent winters
dust and summer heat.
You must light me
with your careful
carried up candle
at night, for I by
myself am dark.
But then I will give you
your shadow back.'

So I came and
brought a chair and
an old kitchen table.
The marks of the rolling pin
were on it and the tiny ruts
of the chopping knife.
It had worked with the old woman
all her kitchen life
and in the drawer were
one or two scribbled notes
when I found it.

And I came again
with piles of old scrap
paper and a pen, some
coloured inks (a pretty thing)
a bottle with a light
an extra coat. O and
the portraits of some
writers (for encouragement).

I drummed my wooden
fingers on the table
dipped my pen into
the unstirred paint pot
of the imagination
and began.

'Yes, a figment of the romantic imagination'
I say, disparaging.
The coloured inks are sitting pretty on my tongue
like wine
but I want to go home.

Notebook

One thing about keeping a notebook is that it fosters the habit of writing in small chunks, unrelated to each other, held together only by the covers of the book and the life threading its way in and out between lines.

'Today I bought a new pair of tights from Woolworths' and two days later 'I glued my tights to my leg trying to stop the hole running into a ladder. They ripped when I took them off. I suppose I shall have to buy another pair.'

Many women keep diaries, scribbled while the washing steams or the potatoes boil, always in snatches. There is never time for the words to boil over into stories, never time for the dream to grow in its slow wilful way. The husband wants his slippers put out to warm by the fire, or Eve is calling, Sarah's been sick all over the bed, it must have been those liquorice sticks . . . And now she'll have to soak the sheets in the bath and cuddle Sarah, giving her all the tenderness she needed to coax her slow hesitant tale into being.

And so, in snatches . . . 'I'm so tired today' and 'He's worried but he won't tell me what it is' and 'Matty needs a new tunic for school. The old one's split right down the pleats at the front. So threadbare this life. Potatoes and gravy.'

a poem for my mother

the sky is the quiet blue
colour of mary's faded cotton frock

carpenter's wife picking the splinters
out of her husband's fingers

and I am thinking quietly
about you

who played Chopin
less perfectly than Rubinstein

I remember your difficult bits
as if somewhere the grass got into a knot

or the moon cricked her neck very slightly
and everything was all right

clockmender's wife picking the cogs and wheels
out of the boiling pan

before the sky walks quietly
into another ordinary dawn

winter among the skips

you often said
there was a garden
where someone picked roses
played at god

somewhere the council
carried out its work of demolition

poking in skips
on sunday afternoon
we found a blue door that had been
the gate into the garden
of number fifteen
paradise walk

how they must have talked
of heaven
when they named that street
and others like it

we put the door in the back of the van
broke it up between us
stacked it in pieces
ready to burn

inspecting the ashes
with the brush and dustpan
the morning after the fire

we had been talking of summer
walking for hours among roses

between slats of the grate
I uncovered the hinge of the garden gate
unclappered it was
strange how I found
no earthly use
for it now

there is no gate
to the garden of illusion
cynical we sit about
discussing rehabilitation

throw bits of old doors
to the fire
to warm our toes
in winter

once upon a time
someone sat in the garden
in paradise walk
on sunday afternoon
by the rosebed
enjoying a sunday talk

that was what you said

four

In the Dark

A cock crows in the hollow night
cracking his false dawns
knucklebones
to the great bone of the first light.
A squawk in the dark
is not enough to make the morning sing.

I squawked when they slapped me. Sing,
they said, but I was not born.

There is night in my bones that swallows
    everything.

The cold moon was my mother.
Her thin cusp slipped between my lips.
Her breasts were like pearls, white stones.
There is no milk in my bones.

Moonshine cools in the air.
I turn to touch. She is gone.
My lips are bloodless in the blue of no dawn.

Who was my father?
I think he crowed his conquests to the big black
    night
and went down in the sea.

There is no seed in my bones, nothing grows there,
and there is no light.

So long have my nerveless bones
lain watching false dawns
make mock
of the cock's crow. Sing, they said,
for the first light's birth in the bones,
but I squawked
unnerved
in the dark.

Cameo

Mother of amber,
in the shallows of your eyes
a limber love lies
still. Stone animal
that never cries.

Wife Crumbling a Biscuit into her Tea

I know why we invented God –
the Holy Ghost to fill the cracks in air,
an immanent Christ, caress in the wind
when your hand no longer lifts my hair.
We always wanted
love without reserve of bitterness,
tea without leaves to tell the next catastrophe.
But now I see the godhead in a cloud of words and
    old men's musings.
Shall I fetch down the alabaster bust
and dust it,
polish the eyeballs, sedulous,
incredulous still from childhood?

How shall I repair the rent in my threadbare soul?
Can I cobble it?

We have the capriciousness of love to contend with,
that it slips the jesses
suddenly soars towards cloud, hoping the sun lies
    beyond.
I cannot hold you,
all my care come down to a twist of silk that ties
    your foot,
a shoelace in a knot,
a meal, a tidy bed and the same tired body
    brightening up.

There is a dead bird on the garden path
and I cannot get past it.

Love is plaster of Paris. Forgotten honeymoons
bob on the water like paperbags
or Chinese balloons without meaning.
This year we missed the Whitsun fair on the heath,
but I heard laughter held tight in the wind.

I cannot swallow the truth of sleep.

Sometime you were a tongue of fire in my mouth.
Now on winter nights, drained of sound,
I strain for the holiness of ghosts,
awaiting a word from the dream that worries your
sleep.
Love's body turned:
it was never your back that wanted me.

Whatever we invented, carefully loved, and lost
was a brief snatch of sun, a patch on a polished floor
or love-in-a-mist in the bed by the creaking garden
door
or the wind.

Today there is only the black and bitter salvation of
tea.

mother you never told me how to mend
the invisible hole   the soul
worn thin with wondering

all the world's a sheet
and all the women in it   here to turn
sides to middle   when it gets torn   to begin
all over again with a snitch of thread

mother I cannot lie down in this bed   riddled with
    stitches
the pinned bones of the spine itch

it does not do and it does not do
to sit all day and sew

the light of another world filters through
these bare threads

the eye of the needle opens wide
to admit me

'. . . there was a path going to a house . . . inside the house a room with someone in it . . . and a door . . . in the back of the room.' Kate spoke half in sleep.

Eve knew better than to ask 'Who was it? What room?' She waited, sitting on the edge of the hard cane-seated chair by the bed. She went on holding her mother's cold hand, lightly stroking the loose skin. Waiting. She wanted to shift position. The edge of the chair dug into her flesh. She felt the deep red grooves along the backs of her legs.

'Mummy, can I get down now? I don't want any more and it's so boring sitting here.' Eve was fidgety.

'Wait till I've finished,' said her mother. 'If you had to keep stopping to pour out more cups of tea, you'd be a long time too. Besides, it's good for you to learn a little patience.'

Eve glared at her mother's hands spreading a patch of butter on the corner of a slice of bread. Why couldn't she butter the whole thing at once?

Eve held her breath and the clock ticked. One of the curtains blew in a little way and then came to rest. There wasn't much wind outside. It was August.

'This is how I remember it as a child,' her mother murmured. 'On the farm in Suffolk. I used to go out to the fields as soon as breakfast was over to escape Grandmama – your great grandmother, Eve. I spent all day there playing with my doll. I could only take one doll on holiday, and John took his aeroplane. I didn't know what else to do, I wasn't allowed to do much. They were always so busy in the back kitchen skimming milk, making butter. Grandmama often threatened to lock me up in the churn if I wasn't good. And I believed her. John went out in the fields all day with the men. I hadn't got him to play with or stick up for me. And my mother – Gran – spent all day talking to the aunts about other uncles and aunts. There were so many of them.'

'I know,' said Eve softly. Elinor and Bertha and Molly and Daisy and Frank and George and the one who was killed in the war and the youngest one, the one you always said was a bit odd. Didn't he die young?'

'Yes, that's right. He was another John.'

They were on familiar ground now, though for Eve familiar only in imagination. She had been to the old home farm once, when she was quite old, fifteen or so, during a family holiday. But it had passed into strange hands by then and they hadn't gone in, only sat in the car a few minutes by the gate in front of the rather stern grey house. The garden was still, the windows all shut. Parlour and best bedrooms only. All the life was round the back in the farmyard, by the big kitchen door that opened in two halves, where there were lots of cats and chickens, and red-faced men in wellington boots. They hadn't seen any of that. Eve only knew it was all happening where they weren't allowed to go now, and then they had driven on to look at the church in Lavenham.

'All right, *now* you may get down,' said Kate, exasperated.

The three of them wriggled down from dining room chairs and tore at the apron strings at the back of their necks and middles. Difficult places to untie things.

'Mummy, why do we always have to wear aprons?' grumbled Sarah for the umpteenth time.

'You know why. To save me so much washing.'

'But *I* never spill anything. Matty does 'cos she's only a baby.'

'I'm not,' declared Matty, as she did many times every day, 'and when I'm big I'll be bigger than you. So there.'

It was true. Matty was a sturdy little thing. She took after Kate's own mother. The other two were skinny, fragile, nothing of the Kings in them at all.

Kate sighed as she fiddled with the sticky knots at the back of three small necks that wouldn't be still.

'Go on now,' she said and they disappeared into the garden. They were suspiciously quiet, but she would have another cup of tea before going to investigate.

Now Eve got up.

That house and someone in a room with another door, was gone. She'd never heard her mother talk of it before. Suffolk was always the same: the farm, Great Grandmama and the butterchurn, Yorkshire pudding and gravy *before* the main course, Yorkshire pudding with a dozen eggs in it, Kate's mother and sisters talking all day and her own solitude and everything tending to show that Kate was 'a funny little thing' – who, however, always proudly added 'I decided when I was quite young I was never going to be a farmer's wife. Such a hard life, and the women count for so little in that world.'

That other house was like a small insignificant picture that no-one ever noticed because it was on the wall just below and to the left of the large brown painting of trees by a summer afternoon river with one or two cows in the foregound. That had pride of place over the untidy sideboard in Eve's Gran's house, where Kate had grown up. The little painting had a black frame and showed a country road at evening, a grey green sky and one or two thin poplars leaning into a wind. A cottage, its windows unlighted, stood in the foregound.

'I'm going to make a cup of tea,' said Eve. 'Would you like some?'

'Yes please,' murmured Kate and closed her eyes against the strong sunlight.

Eve carried the tray across the room and put it down on the big oak box that used to stand in her grandmother's bedroom. She poured out tea and carefully set a cup down on the bedside table. Then she brought a small jug of forget-me-nots she had picked in the garden. She slid one hand under her mother's shoulders.

'Now,' she said gently and together they shuffled Kate up onto the pillows. Kate tried not to groan. Everything hurt her – strong sunshine, the vibrations of even light footsteps across the carpet, someone brushing against the bedclothes. Moving her body was almost intolerable. But a cup of tea would make her feel better.

'Mummy, must I go to school tomorrow?' Eve said in a tiny voice from under the bedclothes. She'd waited until the last possible moment to say this.

'Yes, of course you must, darling. Why don't you want to go? I thought you were doing so well,' said Kate, trying to make her voice reassuring.

'It's Miss Skinner. She's always telling me to walk up straight and not look on the ground. And I can't, I don't know what to do when she shouts "Shoulders back, head up!" '

'Oh, don't take any notice, she won't hurt you.' Kate sighed inwardly over her timid daughter. She *was* round-shouldered, it was true. It worried her now and then, but Eve would grow out of it. She was scared, just like Kate herself had been at that age.

'You're lucky, you know,' Kate said, stroking the curly head on the pillow. When I was your age I had to have a whole year away from school because of rheumatic fever. I missed so much. When I went back I was put in the class below my old one and even so I felt I'd never catch up.'

'What was it like having rheumatic fever?' asked Eve, wanting to keep her mother there, to put off the moment of being left alone in the dark with only the door ajar and the landing light to keep Miss Skinner at bay.

'Oh, I don't remember much about it. I was only ten. I had to lie on my back for months and months. There weren't any drugs then. At first it hurt so much that when anyone just walked across the room I wanted to scream, but I was too weak. Later, when I was better, I was terribly bored and wanted to go back to school. For a long time I wasn't allowed to run or do gym or swimming . . . And then they sent me away to the country to convalesce, all on my own, to Aunty Mildred and Uncle Phil.'

'Did she give you half-a-crown every day?' asked Eve. She knew the story and the answer to this question very well.

'No, she was very strict with me, not like she is with you. She was younger then, she had no children of her own, at least I think . . .'

Eve was asleep. Kate sat on in the small dark room for a while, listening to her daughter's quiet breathing.

A strange feeling about that house and convalescent holiday had remained with her. It was absurd that she somehow couldn't be sure whether Aunty Mildred had had any children or not. There was something funny, something her mother had talked about with the aunts on the farm each summer, something in hushed voices that went on while she was somewhere else or was reading, that stopped abruptly when they realised she was there. There was someone called Monica . . . Oh, she'd never got it straight.

Quietly Kate got up and went downstairs.

Kate was often better in the evening, when the sun had gone down below one hill and above the others the sky was pale green and one or two stars came up. Then she talked in a stronger voice.

'You know,' she said that evening, when Eve had taken the washing things away and was there again to sit beside her until she slept, 'there were so many things I wasn't allowed to do. All my childhood I think I spent wriggling out of the big strong hands of my mother and the aunts – they were all big women – and running away from the butterchurn . . . And then there was needle and thread. Your Gran was a wonderful needlewoman.'

'I know,' said Eve softly. 'She made all those frocks with frills and white collars and cuffs for us, and I always wanted to wear trousers.'

'And I couldn't sew – you know I still can't. I used to stop in mid-stitch and let my grubby dressing-table mat fall on the floor and watch her embroidering huge red poppies and cornflowers on tablecloths. So sure her hands were, the way they held the frame under the material, the way the Crewell needle never stopped going in and out until it was time to get tea . . . I wasn't allowed to have a bicycle and go up on the common to look for rabbits, like John was.'

Eve smiled ruefully. 'We weren't allowed to have bikes either, or play out in the street.'

'But the traffic was so much worse by the time you came along,' answered Kate, 'and besides, you usually seemed content with the garden. You used to spend whole days behind the trellis. That was your house – the arch in the trellis the front door, wasn't it?'

'No, the back door,' said Eve, 'opening straight into the kitchen. And the garden path was a path across fields leading up to the house. And we always let the dolls play out in the fields wherever they wanted.'

Kate smiled. 'But you wouldn't let them go through the door at the back of your kitchen, would you?'

'Well no, of course not,' said Eve. 'That led into the lane at the bottom of the garden and you were so firm about us never going out there, we could hardly let the dolls do it, could we? I remember we told them stories when we put them to bed. We said that door led into the parlour and nobody ever went in there, except at Christmas. The rest of the year there was a strange thin woman in there who ate half crowns and nothing else. There were jam jars full of them in the corner cupboard. I think we must have had Aunty Mildred in mind. We scared the dolls, we could see them get paler, Daisy and Elinor and Molly and Bertha. We said she would laugh her queer rattling laugh and catch them up in her bony hands and twist their feet so they couldn't run and make them sit still for ever more.'

Eve stopped. Kate had closed her eyes. Her face looked drawn all of a sudden. Perhaps she would die quite soon.

'Yes,' said Kate, her voice rather remote. 'That room, there *was* someone in it. That room that led out of the kitchen – the window of that room was at the front of the house. She told me never to play in the front garden because of the flowers. Big red roses, poppies and geraniums. But there were some tiny blue ones too, forget-me-nots, I think. I wanted to make a little bunch of flowers for Betty, my doll, one day, one afternoon when they were asleep. I crept round the side of the house and tried to open the wooden gate into the garden. But it was shut tight, nailed up probably. They never used it. I had to go back through the yard and down the lane to the road where Aunty Mildred had told me never to go because of the tractors. I climbed over the big front gate and started up the path, stopping after every two or three steps because the gravel crunched. The forget-me-nots were under the window, the casement to the right of the front door. I crept right up to the door, waited in the porch a moment, holding my breath. The paint was cracked, I picked at it with my finger nail, got a big flake off, broke it between my finger and thumb. Nothing moved. So I crept out and round to the window, balancing on the bricks that edged the flowerbed so as not to leave any footprints in the earth. It was difficult. I nearly lost my footing and grabbed at the windowsill and just then in the crack left open between the heavy green curtains inside that window I saw something move against the dark of a door in the opposite wall – a pale hand put up to a pale face. I froze. Then I dipped down, crouched on the flowerbed, forgetting about footprints. I hadn't seen it, I hadn't, I didn't know anything. I'd been up in the apple tree by the stable all afternoon talking to Betty, telling her never to go round the front of the house because of the ghost . . .'

Eve waited. Her mother's white face merged into the pillow in the blue grey half dark. She wanted to know, she'd always wanted to know.

'Tell me,' she said fiercely inside herself. 'Don't sleep, don't die. I want to know who it was. I want to know who you are.

'Little mother inside the big one. Like a Russian doll. I always wanted one of those, but they were expensive and you said after all what could you do with them but unscrew them and set them out in a row on the table and find that the littlest inmost one was the same as the outside one. You couldn't unscrew the littlest one, so what was the point? Better to have real dolls you could dress and wash and put in a pram and take out for a walk.

'You were always so busy with making tea and buttering bread and mending our dresses and telling us stories. The world was all right and safe and Miss Skinner could squawk in the dark and not lift a finger to straighten our scared round shoulders. You always said it would be all right and though the skin was loose on the backs of your hands and they ached in the hot summer weather and you suffered and I was annoyed that you should ever feel pain, still your hands put the sometimes broken world together again and untied difficult apron strings and spoke of Suffolk and mythical Yorkshire puddings . . .

'But maybe you never knew either, were never allowed to know. Why have you never told me before this story about the house with the room with the door in the back? And why did we always know about it anyway?

'The dolls are up in the junk room now, Daisy and Bertha and Molly and Elinor. They are sat in a row on an old wooden bench and they're pale from so much washing and so many years ago. But the skin will never be loose on the backs of their hands, their feet stick up, their arms are open, waiting to be held, they smile. One day they'll have to go.'

Kate was asleep. Eve gently let go of her hand and went downstairs to the kitchen. It was dark.

'Mummy, come and look. We've made the dolls

die. Look, we put white paste in their mouths. They've died of diphtheria because when they were born there weren't any injections like we had.' Eve pulled impatiently at her mother's hand.

'Now, Eve and Sarah and Matty,' said Kate, 'why on earth have you done that?'

Notebook

When the train enters the tunnel my stomach knots and my heart beats much too fast. And when it stops I want to scream to break the silence that closes in, to shatter the walls that surge in on me, pressing their terrible weight, squeezing the air I must breathe not to die, constricting my throat. But I cannot scream or they will laugh at me and my scream will rip open the seams of my skin and I shall grow formless, my consciousness dispersing to bang its myriad senseless heads on the implacable walls of the tunnel.

the partygoer (self portrait)

no-one can doubt these dancers
they are big as trombones

(but who is this undecided
one

whose heart is a ragbag
of irregular beats

whose words are halfpennies
belonging to anyone

who is afraid to be
today

but holds yesterday
crumpled tight

like a paper handkerchief
no-one can straighten out

who would slip the remains of her life
onto anyone else's plate

and nip out
for some cigarettes)

no-one can doubt these dancers
they are bright-eyed as flutes

All the small grey words huddled behind the huge black scream. They had tried to quell this monster, to keep it down. Grey ash lava at the mouth of the volcano, they had been trembling for years, centuries, millenia. They had chattered incessantly, applying their palliatives – reason, sanity, consistency, morality, form, dignity, complexity, diversion, intellectuality – to the great red wound. They had gathered in a fearful crowd around the edges of the hole. They had pawned themselves against the explosion, knowing always that this was to no avail. It had to come, the blood, the splattering scarlet blossom, the leaping fire, the surging flood.

The monstrous scream surged up, black, overwhelming, enveloping. Tornado, it caught the small grey words in its great wind whirl, scooped them up, buffeted and hurled them round and round and round again in its centripetal insanity, scattered the senses out of them as it tore them inexorably into the dark hot centre at the base of its axis, then dropped them suddenly, still. The scream turned itself slowly, slowly, slowly gathering speed, unravelling itself into a streaming laughter that hurled about the air, filling the atmosphere with particles of laughter, globules of black sticky laughter swirling and tumbling like a black snowstorm that gradually came to settle, slowing, glutinous, choking the shivering senseless words, blacking them out.

Now there was only a blackness of laughter, filling the air, covering the whole land, turning and turning upon itself, revelling in the vast emptiness it filled. Black, viscous, becoming liquid, it fused into itself, writhing in its existence, spreading, spreading and growing until it had become all there was. It burst into spontaneous combustion, all of it at once. There was vastness of fire, all flames, leaping, many many hued, burning and leaping and licking. It burned itself out, subsiding into nothingness, flickering out into dissolution.

In the freshness of a new air, cold and coming from nowhere like the wind, the little words roused themselves, woke up, and found that they were no longer grey, but crimson, blue, yellow, green, many hued, all the colours of the rainbow, newborn, but whole, childish, full of themselves and of all the newness that there is.

Dilatation and Curettage

(St. Bartholomew's
Hospital, ECI
Winter 1978/9)

out patient

do not enter me tonight I said –
the cold steel of the speculum –
a doctor's casual hands
                    in plastic

I thought I had at last got back
my womb my own soul's cradle quietly
rocking me awake – the awkward bits
of body that were never mine –
flesh I pared to find a bone –
an angularity – an elbow to withstand
the greedy clammy hands –
blunt instrument the speculative eye of man –
and cunt the round dark pool inside the sea
the ark – am I incoherent?

I walked out
          with clitoris
          and cervix
          and vagina
severally intact
a walking diagram
of how to put a cap in
for example
          or a tampax
I was all that

but do not come inside me now tonight
for I am a boat cast up –
an empty vessel – I can tittle tattle
like a woman – I could even be hysterical
but I am not

in patient ___________________________

I am
in case they should lose me somewhere in the sea
and I should never float back up
a name spelt out along a strip of plastic
on a wrist

the wrist belongs to me

you kissed me then
I couldn't take you with me
on the voyage out
they only let you say goodbye
and briefly take a hand
into your own unwritten one
and hold it
              you were still
              someone without a name
              someone choosing a star

I was going
but the student doctor
grappled with a form
                          odd facts
about my body's history
                          and allergies
and all my awkward questions
                          so that he forgot
to get my signature

but did he understand
exactly what it means
never to accept an answer?
he wanted me to smash
a crock of doubt
to smithereens
and let a sea of
makeshift certainty
come in

there was an argument
the doctor half bit back his anger
watched me sign away my portion of forever

there and the other woman was putting
her brief life history into my hands
too far gone into nowhere to hold
her husband, one beloved son
some rooms in a high rise block, a bicycle
a round of well meant meals on wheels
and Hackney
what was that – a star, an island
in a sea without horizons?

'they say' she said
and told me women's tales of blood

there was the journey overland
a trolley crossed a desert
with my body on it
                                        there were corridors and lifts
and down inside the bowels of building was
a kitchen and potatoes cooking endlessly
with mince
                                        and other bodies
wheeled along on trolleys
                                        solitary ships
their sails tucked in
                                        that almost
touched and let a smile slip
                                        from the frightened figurehead

and sometimes here and there
my spirit stepped out
from this straitened body
                                        with a question
metaphysical deliberate and difficult

death I shall carry with me all my life
putting up with it
like a hole in the heart

that's where the sea will come in
when I go down
and don't come up

but this time
I'll come up for air again they say
but where shall I have been?
'it's only twenty minutes now' they say
what does that mean?
is it a ship's watch
or shorter? is it as long
as the life of a fish or a star?
how far shall I have been –
over the watery moon
or only hiding under the green spar
of a sunk galleon?

shall I say simply
I have not been
and it was only
my body's unimaginative breath
a ghost in a machine
would not let me
cry death?

at last to the end of such dry land we came
and in the anteroom were
painted ducks upon a painted pool
upon an ocean of blue wall
                                        where I would go down
and birds flew off across
a ceiling of blue sky
                                        I was
not fooled. these were the souls
of the faithful departed perhaps
and I would accept no hope

but a nurse smiled like the sun
                                        remote and dutiful
and asked if all my teeth were gone
while someone put the needle in
and
                                        did a duck squawk then?

here are stars where I dissolve
a capsule soluble in water anywhere
                    someone
fizzles out into the dark
                    no-one
cares where she is gone
                    or where
in the sea she'll come down

there is a body on a table

and the bird is flown
out of this rapidly dilated womb

and then they called it afterwards
I went along with that
                    and clocks
and the long trek back on a trolley
parts of which did not occur
                    I know they
hauled me up an empty boat
onto a bed of sand
and bid me sleep
which I did not
                    there was no argument

I held the secret
of the dark like
a silver fish
in my hand

much later
after scrambled egg and toast
they pulled a needle out
of a hand
and brought a list
of do's and don't's
to take home
and gave me back my name

what was it for?

you came and kissed me then
and woke me to a world
of Tuesday afternoon
and rain and Islington
as we walked out
I knew the same old
hole in my boot
would let the water in

out patient

return to the hospital

small face fixed in
the old uncertainties

fierce for the doctor

what will the evil eye of the speculum see?

but the casual hands are busy with paper
shuffle the usual questions

'no need to disturb you again
is everything fine?'

I affirm the old pain

was I ever a woman
silent and beautiful?

clasp to me quietly
my womb
like a reticule filled with
such fragments of being
as I have been able to
bring together

odd beads of coral
one of the further stars caught
unexpectedly in the corner of
an eye, a sea anemone
the moon's sad mouth
rolled up like a lady's glove
a coracle roughly woven
of love and tried by
a winter sea
a silver fish

'we do not wish to see
you back'

pick up my small bits and walk away

and after all I said ______________________

I wonder where I have been

and if I ever had a name

but you who have known me
come in now

for I return
begin to try
and tell you
who I am

Notebook

My period has come again today. Since the D and C it has arrived with remarkable regularity. On the nineteenth of the month. I think they inserted a small clock when they scraped me out. Now I conform to the books of theory about women. Except that it is still not twenty-eight days. And February will fool them. It won't come on the nineteenth of March. The calendar is riddled with the muddle of the lunar month. Leap year is a makeshift solution. Poor men with their linear time stretching away into an infinity that defeats the imagination. They don't understand that it all goes round and round, going away and coming back like the moon. Womb lining going away and growing soft and rich and full again only to go away. But the baby they say that is the point of it all. To make another son. Or another daughter who will make another son. But it isn't the point at all. It is only the graspable segment of the cycle, the full and obvious moon. The rest is invisible. The odd little ache of ovulation. The texture of juices changing through the month. The thin long wet one clear and inviting as a river on a hot day. The clagged sticky white stuff that dries in the air. The rains and the drought of desire. They are not aware. A lubricating jelly disguises these differentials. Vagina is always there to be pushed up into. Moon is always there, visible or not, to be landed on.

five

Self Portrait

A woman is painting a cup and saucer patiently.
She is waiting for tea.

a letter to you on the first sunday in september

last year this day shone

this morning I happened to write the date and
    remember it

though we were only in cheltenham
garden of england   nothing like eden I imagine

we began to remember one another
without a shadow of doubt

though the earth was beautiful with shadows
    under the trees
as we walked out

there have been hundreds of london days to help us
    forget this

after the summer of rain
there were apples   so many hopeful suns
    everywhere
pears like young moons   grains of light in the
    long grass

walking about in the dark of this last year
morbid with shadows   unremembering   I
    happened
upon this day   shining

in limbo

it is something old, something
new, something borrowed,
something blue. it is
unwed, always
separable, footloose,
ignorant as a shoe.

it is a mended nightdress
folded flat
without a dream
to warm and crumple it.

it is the rumpled bed
of a departed lover
and may be sorrowful.

it is a stained sheet
washed again.

it is stretched like a
winter vest, tucked
in to itself,
a glove.

it is torn by love
but flexible, hopeful
under the sun.

it is a human skin
to wrap a human in.

Five women sat in the room, in a rough circle on the floor. The clear light of a summer evening came in through a high open window. Four of them had been there before and the fifth one said,

'My name is Mary. Who are you?'

They went round the circle.

'Margaret.'

'Jo.'

'Eve.'

'Katy.'

'Have you all been coming to the workshop a long time? What do you do?'

They looked at each other, waiting for someone to speak. Margaret smiled and said,

'We bring in our poems and, if there aren't too many of us, each person reads her poem in turn and we talk about it. We usually bring copies, without them it's difficult to discuss the poems seriously and in detail.'

'Well, I've brought a poem but I'm afraid I didn't think of making copies. Yes, I suppose it *is* a good idea.'

'Don't worry – we'll probably ask you to read it twice,' put in Katy. 'Well –' She looked round. 'Shall we start?'

There was silence.

'I haven't brought anything this week, I'm afraid. It's half term and the kids have been at home,' said Margaret apologetically.

'I started last week,' put in Jo quickly. 'Eve, what about you? You didn't read last time.'

Eve rummaged in her bag, drew out a sheaf of papers and passed them round. Her hand shook slightly and she lit a cigarette while they read through the short poem. She read it aloud. There was silence. She smoked fervently. She was unsure about this poem, she awaited their comments anxiously.

Jo eventually broke the silence.

'I'm not happy with the first three lines,' she said reflectively. 'It's all those "somethings", they're, they're . . .'

She gesticulated, trying to work out with her hand what she wanted to say.

'Perhaps you could cut out all but the first one,' suggested Margaret. She read out the lines without the stifling repetition.

'Yes, that sounds fine,' approved Katy.

Eve was thinking about it.

'Yes, she said slowly, 'I think it would be better . . . What about the last two lines? Aren't they rather trite, too much of a punch line? I was thinking of –'

'Bye Baby Bunting,' smiled Katy.

'No, I like it – but then I don't like to be left in the air,' said Margaret.

'I was pleased when I got it,' said Eve. 'Before that I wasn't sure what I was writing about – a shadow, a skin, some sort of container, but without an identity, that was the important thing.'

'I like "and may be sorrowful".'

'Yes.' Eve took up Margaret's words eagerly. 'The skin gradually comes more alive as the poem goes on. It gets capable of more emotion. At first it's lost, ignorant, footloose, it can't relate, then it's just a nightdress, it isn't even able to dream. But then when it's the bed, it's not sure, but it might be unhappy. Much later it has been torn by love.'

'I think "torn" is too strong,' said Mary, able to join in now. She tried to explain. 'It seems too dramatic, irrevocable.'

'No –' Eve picked up the last word. 'It's torn like the nightdress. It's been mended, it can go on.'

'I like the domestic imagery,' broke in Katy. 'It's really a woman's poem. They're such nice, ordinary things – a sheet, a vest.'

'For me, it makes things human and manageable,' said Eve. She was thinking aloud now, she wanted to pick up on her previous train of thought. 'It's been hurt, this human skin, but it finds it can go on. It can't start all over again, it's stained and washed, torn and mended, it's old and new, it can never be pure again, but it's learned to be flexible, to pick itself up, to be hopeful . . .' She fell silent, she knew she was talking about herself in the guise of the skin. She knew the other women were aware of that, were giving her the space and the support she needed to do it.

The room was quiet.

'I do like it,' delared Margaret.

'So do I, very much,' added Mary.

'O good,' smiled Eve. 'Now I'll go home happy!' She spoke wryly, half joking. She needed their support, she needed this workshop where they all tried to be critical but helpful at the same time.

' "Under the sun" teases my memory,' she added. 'I know it comes from somewhere – probably Shakespeare, I think . . .'

'Somebody's raisins are ripened "under the sun",' teased Katy.

'O no,' returned Eve, mock serious. 'It's much more impressive and cultural than that.'

'*King Lear*,' suggested Mary.

'Yes,' said Eve, 'or *Antony and Cleopatra*.'

Several days later Jo sent her a letter. 'It's not *King Lear*,' she wrote. 'I'm starting on "Antony and Cleo" today . . .'

a woman observed in winter

at the heart of the windquick wood
you are quiet and beautiful
a bare embroidery of winter tree

bone needles thread
the starred and silent sky

and in your hair
the rare sharp sun of winter
struggles like a bird

you cast tangled threads and shadows
of a summer thick with the big red
outburst of roses
in a quiet hedgerow

for a friend gardening

today you are
digging over your thoughts
like an autumn garden   imagining
next spring   as a lawn
for stretching out
a new person

Gift of Red Flowers

You woke me up
with your red buds of flowers
that opened and asked me

Why did I sleep still, sheathed in green,
when the sun came
seeking the quick of me?

spring

every bone of my body
in bud

It was a tender thing. She wrapped it up and kept it warm in her heart. She wrote poems to Luisa and it was in the poems.

Luisa came from Malaga in Spain. She was the last of fourteen children. She walked in the orchard with her old tired mother. She loved the fruit trees before her father sold the land, keeping only the small vegetable garden behind the cottage. Apricots shone in her eyes. She also came from Barcelona where she wandered the streets of the old city making up poems about the dark earth. She was a student of philology, but lazy. Her friends said she should tighten up her poems, they dreamed too much.

She came to live in London and could not learn the English language. It was too squat, it cut her short. She made friends with some Spaniards, some Argentinians, laughed with them, drinking wine in the long grey-dark nights. She found work in a club, a restaurant, a Spanish cafe. Someone lent her a bicycle to go home on at three o'clock in the morning, when the dancers and drinkers had left and the manager yawned and divided the paltry tips among the thin waitresses.

She was thin. She dreamed as she ate. Life was a magical thing, but not filling. She had an orange for breakfast and a small cup of strong black coffee.

She cooked on a gas ring in the narrow room someone had lent her while he went to India. She invited Margaret and Eve on a Sunday afternoon and made them Spanish omelette, cooking it like her mother did, and fruit salad and honey. She watched over them as they ate.

'More, Eve, eat more,' she laughed, cutting a great slice of omelette and lifting it onto Eve's plate.

Eve was shamefaced.

'I am always so hungry,' she said, regretting her appetite.

'But you are so thin.'

'My mother always says I have hollow bones.'

They looked at Margaret who smiled and translated 'hollow bones' into Spanish. Luisa smiled too, admiringly.

Eve tried to narrow her wide square shoulders as she attacked the second helping of omelette. She felt clumsy.

She watched Luisa as she moved gracefully, quietly in stocking feet, between the stove and the fireplace, serving them coffee. Her hair was almost black and very long, it mantled her shoulders and her back. She sat down on the floor, cross-legged and still, expectant, her eyes shining behind thin round spectacles.

They took out some poems. Luisa rolled herself a cigarette, slowly, meditatively.

They met to read their poems to one another – Eve and Luisa and Margaret, who translated them each to the other. Eve listened anxiously to her own close worked lines, their terse concentration freed into the soft lilt of Spanish, beginning to flow. Luisa laughed, her responses spilled over in Spanish. Eve wanted to stamp her foot when Margaret replied to Luisa before translating.

Eve came to know how her poems grew out of the language she spoke and heard spoken around her every day; how they were colloquial; how they relied and drew upon the old sayings and common sense phrases she had grown up with; how they played on all the possible meanings of words in a language complex and flexible. It was Luisa who gave her that understanding. She was grateful and she despaired. She was trapped in the language that created her world. How could she and Luisa ever come together, merge and submerge themselves in one another?

Yet Luisa remained untroubled.

'I love your poem about the old grandmother,' she said. 'I took it to work every day for a week and translated it on the tube, more lines every day, until I had it. Your poems make me want to work at my English.'

Eve was humbled by her candour, her trust.

Luisa's poems told her of a dark rich earth, a shining river, cypresses, the brown lined face of the old peasant woman her mother, the mellow light of a kind moon, the terror of a young friend who wanted to die. They spoke to the things and the people they spoke about and they became them. Her love was a garden of lemon trees, her sorrow a friend without hope, her death the black river in a moonless night.

Eve listened to the strange soft sounds, watched Luisa as she knelt on the floor reading her poem quietly from the thick white sheet of paper on her knee. She listened to Margaret's careful translating, her frequent breaking off to discuss the exact meaning of something in Spanish. She watched her smile as she found the right word, tried to follow the wandering pattern of thought and images.

'Read it again in Spanish!' she commanded. She took the paper from Luisa, looked and puzzled and tried to remember and couldn't and tried to say something responsive, something intelligent. Always she felt inadequate, always the poem slipped her anxious grasp, always she must disappoint Luisa by saying nothing.

Occasionally she questioned Margaret, tried to elucidate the connection between two images in a poem, tried to hold the meaning in her hand like a word made of wood. She felt it was wrong to probe like that. She hoped Margaret would not translate their short discussion.

Luisa's poem was a tree and the tree took root in her heart and started to grow there.

But Eve worried. She tried to just open her eyes and smile that she understood, that she felt the poem inside her. But she couldn't. She was lost without words, her cold counters of communication.

Luisa was tired and cold in London. She decided to go home. The three women met for a last meal in Margaret's house.

It was a strange, subdued, rather silent evening. Luisa was sad. Margaret was caught up in her own worries she would not speak about. Eve was at odds with the world and herself. She had not been able to find her poem places that day, she had lost the flow of the world, her body was stiff, heavy, awkward. She sat hunched on the floor, arms gripped tight round her knees so the skin got red and itchy. She was irritable and wanted to be alone.

Luisa's sadness was too much with her. It was a cool wind in a tall green forest; it was rain dripping from green leaves during a great summer rain; it was a thin path, barely visible, winding on and on into the heart of the forest. She felt the foliage around her, she heard small birds singing in the wet trees. She was walking on her own and she could not turn back.

When Margaret went into the kitchen to season the salad, Luisa came to Eve where she sat and knelt before her. She did not speak, she laid her thin hands on Eve's shoulders, her sorrow looked out of her eyes. They were great dark pools where Eve saw herself, ugly and squat. She buried her head in Luisa's dress putting her arms round the slim fragile body.

She was slight as a bird. Eve was afraid she would crush the bones.

After supper Luisa read them a poem, three pages long. It was a dream poem. Luisa was walking in a great forest and sun came through the trees dappling the mossy ground with pools of silver and gold. She met a woman in a clearing, who was a young sapling, lithe and sinuous, her light pale leaves moving almost imperceptibly in the still green air. When she turned she was made of crystal, cut precisely, granite hard and still, sticking her needles of sun into the breathing shadows.

Luisa read, Margaret translated, Luisa read again. They were silent. Each of them knew the woman. Eve did not ask for the specific meanings of words. She let herself come face to face with the woman of leaves, the woman of crystal.

Perhaps it just happened that Eve and Luisa left together and walked together through the quiet dark square towards Eve's house, which was near. Luisa held her hand, caressed her cold fingers, walked so close beside her, her black hair tickled Eve's cheek. Eve looked up for the moon and found her almost full.

'Look.' She pointed with her free hand, she took a deep breath, she had broken their rhythmical silence.

'She is so far away,' said Luisa, wistful for her own warm land where the moon crept closer to the earth.

They had come to Eve's house.

'I will make you some tea. Can you stay for a while?'

Luisa smiled and let go of Eve's hand while she unlocked the door.

Eve hid Luisa in her room.

'Copy the poem for me, please,' she pleaded, clearing a space on the untidy table. 'I will make tea.' She wanted to escape Luisa's warmth, her sad smile, she wanted to bang cups and teapots and spoons about in the kitchen. But Luisa took hold of her, slipping an arm round her waist beneath her coat.

'Eve, Eve,' she said gently, spinning her slow smile around her. Eve was caught in a gossamer web, held by the two still pools of her eyes. She acquiesced, she kissed her on the lips, she laid her soft cheek against Luisa's. Luisa bent her head, her hair was massed about them, keeping them warm.

Eve broke free, she ran down to the kitchen, boiled up water, threw a handful of crisp green leaves into the pot.

Carefully she carried the two cups upstairs.

Eve knew she must ask Luisa to stay and she wanted to and was afraid. She squatted awkwardly in front of the electric fire, sipped the tea she didn't want, smoked one cigarette after another.

'Eve,' murmured Luisa. 'Why do you smoke so much?'

She was calm, she was full of the quiet of a summer night, she was a tree that moved in a warm wind, its leaves whispering silence.

She took off her glasses, folded them, laid them on the orange-box beside the bed.

Her eyes were like stars in a clear night sky in the country. Her voice was a river flowing deep and slow. Her hands were kind as houses in a solitary place, their lights shining out of small bright windows.

Eve made interruptions. She fetched an atlas, made Luisa show her where she had grown up, made her talk about the farm, made her talk in this abrupt language she found so difficult.

At last she said,

'I think perhaps we should go to bed.'

They lay quite still with their arms round one another. Luisa was content, she smiled up into Eve's face. Small fires danced in her dark eyes, so alive they were with sun and apricots.

Eve looked down on her dark elfin face, the great black mane of her hair spread wide on the pillow like water. Eve let it run through her fingers.

'I always wanted long straight hair,' she said regretfully.

'But your curls, Eve, they are so pretty,' laughed Luisa, pulling them out one after the other, watching them spring back tight.

Luisa was so slight, so fragile. Her breasts were small as grapes. Eve kissed them in turn.

'They are too small,' sighed Luisa.

'And my shoulders are too wide,' sighed Eve.

They laughed at the despairs of womanhood.

'Te quiero,' Luisa said, her eyes filled with a wonder greater than the sky.

'I love you,' Eve returned, but she was ill at ease with the unnecessary words. She had a new feeling that put out its first green shoots in her heart. She lay letting it grow.

They put out the light. They slept in the quiet forest of the night, feeling the trees grow under the stars.

Luisa gave Eve anemones and a big Spanish orange. Eve gave Luisa a tiny silver paperknife she had found in a junkshop. Luisa went home to Spain. Their letters were stilted and difficult, so they wrote one another poems.

this year   a poem for jo

this year
a diningroom table and an upright chair

a piece of paper
to puzzle over   my mirror

what colour
are my eyes   is my hair

outside   cars   so many men have tried
to make a motorway out of my body

but it is a house for are you sitting comfortably in
with velvet curtains

for a whole year you sat in your rocking chair
thinking   like a grandmother

I love you for that
sculling about in the backwaters

of belly and heart   that anchoring
your own rocker

this year   my quiet room   you can count
  on finding
someone at home

In this new garden there is a real apple tree. The top branches are just outside the window of my writing room. Writing room. More here and now than garret. Less romantic. Though in some ways this room is like my old ones in the other house.

There is no electrical socket. I have chosen not to put in a new ring main or even a spur. I have learned these words and I am sticking to an extension lead from another room. The light is unpredictable. Sometimes it works, sometimes not. I don't understand why. Perhaps it simply knows when to rest. Do I know that yet? No matter. I have a table lamp.

Somewhere I know I have a paperback copy of *A Room of One's Own*. On the cover there is a sketch. A table and chair in front of a window. The room must be at the top of the house because the casement is small. The window is open, the curtains blowing. I have set my table and chair in front of the apple tree window. It all looks familiar and now I know why. But I have no curtains. This is a room to work in.

Once it was a kitchen. There was a cooker in one corner. I have disconnected it. Pushed it out onto the landing. I have capped the gas supply pipe. In the plumbers' shop the man snarled 'Yes, darlin'?' I fought back with precision. Trade terms. I have learned to know exactly what I want.

The kitchen sink is still in the room. The lead pipe is cut off at the point where the cold water tap used to be. It is hammered shut, but not quite. It drips, some days fast, some days slow. Odd, the irregularity. I have filled the sink with earth and put in plants. The lead pipe waters them.

The floor is a patchwork of bright lino tiles, many colours. I have done nothing about it. But I have painted the walls blue. On one wall was a patch of bare brickwork, red, the colour of earth in the West Country. I considered this difficult patch for days. I discarded cement, plasterboard, wallpaper, curtains, a cupboard. I am doing without a cover up. Now I've got used to it. I like the shape of it.

I have sorted my papers and put my poetry books in alphabetical order and filled my fountain pen and sat down at my kitchen table. But in this new room I have not had to begin, or even begin again. I am simply going on.

Out there beyond the apple tree, the garden is wild and long. I am looking forward to digging.

Setting Out Lighter

And this word love
we are not likely to use.

Stow it away
like an old school prize

'my first dictionary'

or give it to those
who paddle about
in the pleasure boats
of words.

Love is a curiositie,

the etymology of coming
home

without a history.
You and I

need no candles
to cut loose by.

eve sarah and ruth in winchester, november 1980

only one or two
people   abroad
in the streets
of a winter city
closing down quietly
cauled like a nun
in the cloisters of
god's november light

come two grown women
and a little bone
of their bone

little nun deep
in the habit of sleep

two women
wise in their shoes
walk in the cloisters
over the rows
of important stones
the grave historical
dead

        and alfred
who got his fingers
burnt   taking buns
out of a too hot
oven   is only
a king to tell
a child about
in the fretful
night

little bone grows
like a toe in a shoe

two women skip
a cathedral

slip in and out
of shops that are
stringbags full
of sweet light
they are looking
for bread and
strawberry jam
in the dim
of late afternoon

and little bun warms
towards teatime

Notebook

It has been there for several years. I have started writing it at least three times. I have tried to force it to go on when it didn't want to. It is like a snail that sleeps its slow life away, dreaming its unknowable dream of inside the shell. It comes out occasionally to test the air with its unaccustomed antennae and leaves an almost invisible trail of silver words across the empty page. Then it goes in again. Then one day it comes out and there is my book.

About the Author

I was born in 1949. After two convents, two grammar schools and three years at Cambridge where I studied Philosophy and English, I spent some years unbuckling my imagination and finding enough confidence to write. Since 1976 I have made writing my main occupation. I teach part time in Further Education and sometimes type to make a living.

I was born in London and it feels like home. For the last eight years I have lived in squats, short-life and co-op houses and have put a lot of energy into the politics of alternative housing.

I first got involved in the Women's Movement in 1970. Then there was a gap. Since 1976 I have been more or less actively involved. Without the support of the women's writing groups I have been in – especially the Women's Arts Alliance Poetry Workshop which existed from 1976-1980 – I would probably not have got this book together.